D1525078

THE ENGLISHER

THE AMISH BONNET SISTERS BOOK 6

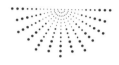

SAMANTHA PRICE

Copyright © 2019 by Samantha Price

All rights reserved.

No part of this book may be reproduced in any form or by any electronic or mechanical means, including information storage and retrieval systems, without written permission from the author, except for the use of brief quotations in a book review.

CHAPTER ONE

*E*verybody would've learned of it by now since her half-sisters knew.

It would've caused a scandal within their Amish community!

Her stepmother would be most upset.

Liza, her best friend, would be shocked.

The bishop and the elders would be disappointed.

Florence hadn't run away. She'd only moved one property over, but she'd certainly escaped from her life with the Baker family.

AT THE BAKER HOUSEHOLD, things weren't running smoothly ever since Florence had left. Timmy, the late Aunt Dagmar's blue budgerigar, had taken to chirping loudly whenever anyone was in the kitchen, and that was most of the day.

"I knew that bird would be trouble," *Mamm* grumbled as she sat at the breakfast table glaring at the poor little bird in his cage.

"Timmy's no trouble at all," said Cherish, who'd been the one to bring him into the home from Dagmar's farm— now, her farm thanks to Aunt Dagmar's will. Cherish plucked him out of his cage and placed him on her shoulder. "There. He just wanted to get out."

Mamm's mouth turned down at the corners. "He's a smelly bird."

"He's not. It's just his cage. And I cleaned it as soon as I got home yesterday. I clean it nearly every day. I don't know why you're so upset." Cherish looked up and she saw Joy frowning at her. Joy thought she was being rude to *Mamm*, but she wasn't. *Mamm* was being rude to her and to Timmy.

"Is the bird really upsetting you, *Mamm?*" Hope asked.

"Of course it is. Everyone knows I don't like birds."

Cherish frowned. "I asked you if I could have Timmy here and you said I could."

Hope agreed, "That's right, she did ask you."

"It was Dagmar's bird and she'd just died. I was put on the spot in the most dreadful way like you girls so often do to me. You already had the bird at the *haus,* Cherish."

Before Cherish could say anything further, Favor spoke.

"He's just a little bird and he makes cheerful sounds and his little chirping noises make me happy."

"That's your opinion," *Mamm* grunted. "I just don't like birds of any kind. Or dogs, and I'm forced to have those two dogs running through the *haus*."

Joy frowned. "Isaac asked you if he could give me Goldie, didn't he? He told me he cleared it with you first."

Mamm narrowed her eyes. "I didn't feel as though I could say no because it was your birthday or some such occasion, but from now on I'm going to have my say around here. I'm going to worry about myself for a change, just the same as you girls do."

"That would be good, think about yourself for a change," Joy said, nodding.

Cherish glared at Joy, the sister who prided herself on being so good. Didn't she know that pride wasn't good at all? All do-gooders were prideful in Cherish's opinion. Didn't pride go before a fall?

"What?" Joy asked when she saw Cherish staring at her.

Cherish put out her finger and Timmy moved onto it. "Why are you always agreeing with her all the time?"

"That would be because she's our *mudder*. We have to respect our parents."

There she goes again, with her constant corrections. "It doesn't mean she's right, and it doesn't mean she can treat us like this, saying yes to things when she really means no. It's confusing. I didn't ask to have a confusing parent. At least

Dat wasn't confusing. He never said one thing when he really meant another." She moved her hand back to her shoulder and Timmy jumped from her finger to her shoulder.

"You're lucky to have any parent at all. I should've adopted you out, Cherish. Five girls were enough for me."

"Don't forget Florence," Favor said.

"Yeah," Hope said. "You had six girls even before Cherish came along."

Cherish couldn't help speaking her mind. She'd never tried to stop saying what she felt and she wasn't going to start now. *"Jah, Mamm,* you should've got rid of me like you got rid of Carter. Tossed him out because he was an embarrassment."

A stunned silence fell over the room, and even Timmy must've sensed the tension because he stopped running from one shoulder to the other.

For some reason, Cherish couldn't stop herself from saying more. "He was a product of your—"

Favor, who was sitting next to Cherish, quickly covered her sister's mouth with her hand. "Don't say it," Favor urged, obviously knowing she'd say something worse.

Mamm jumped to her feet at the same time as Cherish scrambled to hers. She moved so fast that she scared Timmy and he flew back to his cage.

Cherish was about to get a beating and she knew it.

It was something she hadn't gotten in many years.

She was much quicker than *Mamm* and after a quick look to see that Timmy was okay, she managed to race out of the kitchen ahead of *Mamm*.

"I'm going. I'm going to my room," Cherish announced just as she had one foot on the bottom step of the staircase.

Her mother hadn't continued her pursuit and was heading back to the breakfast table. "And you'll stay there all day with no food and no water. See how smart your mouth is then."

Cherish hurried up the stairs, thankful she'd escaped a slapping. She'd gotten a few stinging slaps across her face from her mother over the years. She wasn't the only one; they'd all gotten them in the past except for Florence and her two older brothers, but they were too old to get into too much trouble.

Once Cherish closed her bedroom door, she collapsed onto her bed. Things weren't the same now that Florence was gone. There was no escape for her from this hellhole of a place called home, until she was older. Then she'd live on Dagmar's farm with no one to tell her what to do. She'd be free and could live her life as she saw fit.

She jumped to her feet, walked over to the window and opened it up. Then she stuck her head out and breathed in the fresh air. How she wished things could go back to how they were when *Dat* was alive and all her siblings still lived at home. It had been a happy home back then.

Now everything was a mess.

Literally.

Even the house wasn't as clean and tidy without Florence.

Dat was dead, her older half-brothers were gone, and Florence had abandoned them for love. She didn't blame Florence because she'd do the very same thing if she ever had the chance. Neither would she wait two plus years like Florence had.

She'd run away with a man when she knew she loved him.

Why wait?

Life was short and she intended to live it. And if her life happened to be long, it would be worse to live so many years with regrets.

So many changes were coming. Both Joy and *Mamm* were getting married soon and when *Mamm* got married, Bliss and Levi would move in.

What if Levi thought he could tell her what to do just because he was their stepfather?

What if he gave them more chores, or expected more from them?

That would be just awful.

She never asked for a stepfather and she didn't really get along with Levi. A more boring man she couldn't begin to imagine. He was too quiet and she never knew what he was thinking.

The thing that was especially distasteful was that *Mamm* seemed to go along with whatever he said.

As much as she liked Bliss, her step sister-to-be, she didn't know what her mother had been thinking when she agreed to marry Levi.

She closed the window when a cool breeze swept up.

Just as well her stomach was full from breakfast. She could last all day without eating and by night time *Mamm* would've forgotten her earlier words. She normally didn't carry through with her punishments, not like Florence. Florence was really strict.

CHAPTER TWO

*F*lorence was filled with a mixture of feelings as she stood staring out the window of the cottage she shared with her new husband.

Of course she was delighted to be in love with a wonderful man, but was a little sad when she thought of those who had been inconvenienced by her decision to marry Carter and leave her Amish community.

She'd done her best not to like him and she'd tried to make herself like the Amish pig farmer everyone thought she should marry.

She took two steps back from the window and the morning light fell on the glass pane enabling her to view her reflection.

It was something she'd gotten used to over the last few days, but the image gazing back at her still didn't seem familiar.

Her once long hair now reached just below her shoulders, a far more manageable length. As she moved her fingers to touch some strands, a beam of light reflected off her plain gold wedding band.

A ring was something she never would've worn as an Amish woman. Carter had wanted her to have an engagement ring or at the very least a diamond encrusted band, but she told him she was happier with something more practical. The plain wedding band suited her just fine and he had chosen a band for himself that matched.

The dresses and skirts she wore now were shorter than the Amish dresses, had less fabric, and were a whole lot more comfortable. She found pants comfortable too, but would only wear them for outside work.

Moving closer to the window once more, her thoughts turned to her beloved orchard.

Stretching on her tiptoes, she could see the tops of the first row of trees, and a clearing before the dividing fence. That was all.

She was determined to make Wilma see sense. If Wilma put aside the silly idea of Levi managing it, that would be best for everyone. Except for Levi, but just because he'd finally convinced Wilma to marry him, didn't mean he should take over.

He didn't have the knowledge to run an orchard.

He knew nothing!

Florence groaned aloud and woke up Spot, Carter's dog. He raised his black and white head.

"Sorry, Spot. Go back to sleep."

He put his head back down between his paws and closed his eyes.

The idea of Levi running the orchard upset her just as much today as it had the day she'd first heard it.

The notion was ridiculous, and Florence hoped he knew how to keep the orchard organic and what that meant. There was a strict set of guidelines to keep within.

With the orchard being certified organic, it gave them a point of difference and without that they'd be competing heavily on price rather than quality.

In her heart, she knew Levi would mess things up. Behind his shy demeanor he was a stubborn man. The type who would always figure he knew best.

Before working out how to gain control of the orchard, Florence sat down to write a difficult letter to Earl. She had to tell him her side of things and explain why she'd left the community to marry 'the *Englisher*.'

Things were often best explained in letters where one had the time and the leisure to formulate the exact wording to put across precisely what was in her heart and mind.

Florence wasn't used to talking on the phone. It was uncomfortable not being able to look at the person's face when one was talking. Sometimes people didn't say what they thought, choosing not to hurt the other's feelings, but the eyes and the face couldn't deceive so readily.

As she sat back down on the couch and with pen poised

over the blank page, she wondered as she so often did, why Earl had moved to Ohio so suddenly after *Dat* died.

In the past, it had often confused her that her brothers weren't closer with Wilma, but now that she'd seen a different side of their stepmother, she could totally understand why they'd chosen to leave.

Earl chose Ohio.

Mark chose marriage.

Why else would Mark have married Christina? She was barely polite; her lips were always tight and her expression disagreeable, as though she'd been sucking on something sour.

Her brothers had left her in a household full of women. With Wilma spiraling into a state of mindlessness, Florence had stepped up to take over and become both father and mother.

Florence would've loved to sit around all day like Wilma had, staring into space pondering years gone by and the suddenness of *Dat's* death, but with running the orchard and looking after the girls and the house, Florence wasn't afforded that luxury.

There was work that needed to be done, and someone had to take charge when Wilma hadn't.

She dropped her pen on the paper, moved them to one side, and stood to look out the window once more. It was enough to send pangs of guilt coursing through her body. She'd abandoned her father's orchard. She could've turned her back on love and stayed on, but love—the love she and Carter shared—was so rare and precious that she grabbed it and held onto it with both hands. She hoped *Dat* would understand.

There was still time. Time to work things out with Wilma, for all their sakes.

If Wilma would only think clearly, she'd see that Florence was the best person to run the place.

Florence pushed strands of hair back behind her ears. She still wasn't used to her hair being free. It had spent so many years pinned tight against her head under her *kapp.*

Or was Wilma's choice to put Levi in charge a sign that it was time for her to create a new life of her own, one that didn't include Wilma and the girls?

It would be hard to let go when she knew the girls still needed her.

Two of the girls had already married, and Joy, the third oldest, was due to be married at the end of the year.

The sad thing was her actions would make no sense to her friends and relatives in her community, she was sure of that.

Her mind was pulled back to what outrage the scandal of her leaving to marry an *Englisher* would've caused.

No! Stop thinking about that.

For once in her life, she wasn't going to be concerned about others.

Yes, she was angry with Wilma for keeping her away from

the orchard, but she wasn't going to give up just yet. Not with all the hard work she'd put in and the connection it gave her to her late father.

Still, she had another option if Wilma refused her. She would put everything her father had taught her into her new orchard, the one that she would create together with Carter. She would train up her children to love the orchard just as her father had trained and guided her.

She groaned again at the thought of Levi, and spun around to see Spot's reaction. This time he didn't flinch. He was used to her groans of despair by now.

Florence picked up the pen again and tried her best to explain to Earl in detail the reasons for her leaving.

She wrote about her feelings for Carter, and the fact that she hadn't left God, she'd only left the community.

When she was satisfied she'd explained things the best she could, she signed the letter,

Always your loving sister, Florence.

Without reading it through, she folded the notepaper into three and then placed it in the envelope and licked it closed.

"Carter," she yelled out as she walked to the bottom of the stairs.

"Yes?"

"Will you drive me into town? I want to post a letter."

"Sure. Can you give me half an hour? I'm just in the middle of something."

"Okay. I'll make a cup of coffee. Do you want one?"

"Why don't you wait and we'll have coffee after we post that letter?"

"Good idea." Florence wandered back, sat down next to Spot and patted him.

At her previous home, the Baker family home, she was always kept busy doing something—sewing, cleaning, bookwork, or working in the orchard. Now she didn't know what to do with herself. Her new home with all the electronic gadgets practically cleaned itself. The dishwasher washed the dishes, the electric washing machine cleaned the clothes in no time, and with the dryer, there was no waiting for the sun or the breeze to dry the clothes. It didn't take long to zoom over the floor with the vacuum, either.

She rose to her feet, and wandered to the window and looked out at their few cows chewing on the grass. Carter was attached to his cows and treated them like pets. She couldn't help smiling at the way he was with them. It showed how soft-natured he was.

The cows didn't provide any income, but since Carter was well-off, they didn't have to. Still, he was looking for a new home for his pet cows because they needed the land for their new apple trees—a home where they would be treated properly. If a home couldn't be found, they'd have to keep two paddocks for the cows and go without planting the extra trees. As much as she thought they should go for practical purposes, she wasn't going to insist.

Florence was both excited and daunted by the prospect of creating an orchard from scratch. That was something she'd never done before and she wasn't certain how to go about it. She knew a couple of her father's apple-growing friends would be the best people to ask advice from. Before she drew up plans, she'd visit them. There was one man in particular she wanted to single out for advice.

ON THEIR DRIVE INTO TOWN, Carter made an odd suggestion. "I'll have to teach you to drive a car."

"No, I'd be too frightened. I could never …"

"It's probably easier than driving a buggy, and a lot safer."

Florence wrinkled her nose. "If I take my hands off the steering wheel I'd crash, but if I take my hands off the reins when I'm in the buggy, the horse isn't going to crash into anything. They use their eyes. The car can't think for itself."

"Hmm. Technology is already there in that regard, but we don't have one of those cars." Carter chuckled. "Trust me, it's not hard. I'll get you your own car and then you can come and go as you please. You could drive yourself into town to post your letters. Or—"

"I know. Learn to use email."

He smirked. "I was going to mention that again, but since

you don't know anyone who isn't in the community there's probably not much point." He glanced at the letter she clutched in her hands. "I'm guessing the letter is to Earl?"

"How would you know that?"

He laughed again. "I saw the name *Baker* written on the front of it."

She slapped his arm in mock-irritation. "Stop it. I thought you had some extra powers or something."

"I'm afraid not, but it wouldn't be hard to guess you're writing to your older brother. To explain why you left the community, right?"

"That's correct." She sighed. "I don't know how my family members are going to react or whether they'll disown me completely."

"You'll have to wait and see."

"The waiting part is the worst."

"Don't worry about anybody else, just worry about us. I still can't believe we're together at last. My dreams have come true." He reached out and grabbed her hand.

She was nervous about him driving with only one hand on the wheel. "I can barely believe it either. We're married."

"We are. And I want to make you the happiest girl in the world."

"You already have." She stared at his hands. "But you'd

make me happier right now if you put both hands on the wheel."

He laughed and let go of her hand to clasp the steering wheel. "That didn't take long. You'll be driving in no time. You're already a backseat driver."

"A what?"

"That's what someone's called when they tell the driver how to drive."

"Oh. Well, I can't do that since I don't know how to drive myself."

"Exactly. Backseat driver."

"Safe driver," she countered.

He shook his head. "I've been thinking. I found out about my mother, you should find out more about yours."

"I'd love to. I really would. It was such a surprise to learn she wasn't born Amish. Everything I was told about her led me to believe she was. I mean, no one said anything different so I just assumed ..."

"Don't worry. We'll find out what we can. I know someone who can help."

"I'd like that, but not right now. There's so much going on in my head. Tomorrow I'd like to visit Liza."

"Sure thing. I'll drive you."

"Thank you. After that I'd like to visit some orchards so I can talk with the owners. Two of them were good friends of my father's. I need to ask their advice on preparing the ground, etc. I've never done that. I know what to do after they're planted, but I've never started from scratch. Eric Brosley would be the man who knows the most."

"Sure thing." He parked the car not far from the post office.

She opened the door and then turned to him. "I won't be long."

"I'll come with you. Then there's a coffee shop we can walk to."

"Sounds good. After that, could you drive me to Liza's?"

"Sure thing."

"You don't mind?"

"No. I've got plenty of calls I can make while I wait for you."

CHAPTER THREE

*F*lorence was nervous about seeing Liza. She hadn't told her she was leaving, and normally she told Liza everything. She only hoped Simon wasn't home. Since it was after lunch he should've been at work, and hopefully Liza's two boys would be asleep. Liza might talk to her, or at least allow her to speak, but she wasn't so sure about Simon. She was pretty certain he wouldn't approve. He'd possibly be worried she'd lead Liza astray or put ideas into her head.

Carter left her at the bottom of the driveway where he intended to stay until she finished her visit.

She made her way up the driveway and by the time she got to the door, her heart pounded. She knocked on the door and Liza answered it, and then Liza looked around, over Florence's shoulder. "Florence, I'm so pleased you've come. Are you here by yourself?"

Liza didn't look too thrilled to see her. "I am. I hope I haven't come at a bad time. Have I?"

"Nee, it's a good time. Simon's at work and I've just put the boys down to sleep."

She licked her lips. "Can I come in? It'll only take a moment."

"Of course. Come in."

Florence could feel things had changed between them. It was only to be expected since she'd left the community. It was unreasonable to think that friendships wouldn't be broken. There was a line drawn and Florence had stepped over it by leaving the community.

Liza walked with her into the living room. The atmosphere was more formal than was usual. By now the two of them would've been talking and laughing, sitting in the kitchen while Liza put the teakettle onto the gas stove.

"I'm guessing you've heard?" Florence asked as she sat down, enjoying the aroma of freshly baked bread wafting from the kitchen.

"I have. Everyone's heard, and you're married and everything?"

"I am." Florence could barely believe it herself. She had thought she'd never marry. She reminded herself that nobody knew that Carter was Wilma's child, and she had to be careful. No one outside the family knew and she guessed that's exactly how Wilma wanted it to stay.

Liza groaned. "Oh Florence, I wish you would've talked about it to me first."

"Why, what would you have done?"

"I would've done everything and anything I could to talk you out of it. I don't know why you just didn't marry Ezekiel instead—a *gut* Amish man. There was nothing wrong with him. He would've made you a fine husband."

"Well, if you remember correctly, *he* ended things with *me.*"

"I know and then he regretted his decision and he came back to you. You've told me everything, and you can't fool me. Why did you marry this outsider?"

"His name's Carter."

"I know you might think you're in love with him, but I don't see that as a good enough reason. We're only here for a short time, not to follow our own lusts."

"It's love." Florence was a little disappointed in Liza. She hoped Liza of all people would've understood.

Liza made a face. "Well, we're not to mix with outsiders. We're especially not to marry them. He'll lead you astray. His beliefs will become yours."

"He really has no beliefs."

"That's bad too. He'll influence you."

Liza's marriage had been rocky. "It's hard to explain why I made the decision." Life was short and she'd lived enough of her life without love, but how could she explain that to a woman in a loveless marriage? She had something special that Liza would never have. "You have to live in my shoes to know why I made the decision."

"You're upset with Wilma, is that why you left?"

"I'm in love. That's why I married Carter. It's got nothing to do with how I feel about Wilma. I can't live the rest of my life for Wilma."

"Oh, Florence. What is to become of you?"

"Something good, I hope. I have a new life, new family, and I'm happy."

"To have any redemption, you must have him join us. You must influence him rather than his belief, in nothing, influence you. Will that ever be possible?"

Florence nodded. "That's what I thought once, but haven't you ever thought our way is not the only way?"

"It's a narrow path. If I didn't believe that, I wouldn't be here. Is that why you left us? Has he filled your head with this nonsense about our ways already?"

Florence shook her head. She didn't want to acknowledge it but being around Carter had made her think more deeply about her beliefs, and the Amish *Ordnung* and traditions. Surely there was no harm in that?

"Florence, I don't think you should come back here again. If Simon finds out, I'll be in all kinds of trouble."

Florence knew she was using Simon as an excuse. "Simon? But what do you think?"

"Simon is the head of this household."

"Right, but that doesn't mean you can't have your own opinion about things, does it?"

"I don't want to get into an argument because I'm not good with words."

"I'm sorry, but I wasn't trying to argue. I just miss you, that's all."

Liza bounded to her feet. "I'm sorry, Florence, but we can't be friends while you're outside the community. Please understand."

Florence stood too. She had known she'd lose friends and that the community would turn their back on her. "Well then it looks like I came here to say goodbye."

"I hope you're not upset with me."

"I'm not upset. I understand. I truly do." Florence walked to the door while Liza stayed put.

"I'll pray for your soul, Florence."

Florence turned around and looked at her, just as she reached for the door handle. "Thank you, Liza."

"Are you on foot?"

"No, I have Carter waiting down by the road."

Liza suddenly ran to her and put her arms around her. Florence hugged her too, and then patted her back.

"You've always been the best friend I ever had, Liza." Tears stung the back of Florence's eyes.

"And you'll always be my best friend, Florence. You're the only person I could tell about the problems with Simon because you're the only person I could trust."

The two women parted and Florence walked down the long driveway holding back tears, but she was pleased she'd said goodbye.

WHEN CHERISH'S sisters drove away in a buggy, she heard her mother's bedroom door close. Even though she was supposed to stay in her room all day, it didn't matter. No one would find out she was gone. Now was her opportunity to sneak out.

Her mother's nap normally lasted for at least an hour and her sisters would be gone for ages.

She'd guessed *Mamm was being spiteful and* had sent her sisters into town without her. Everyone knew that she was the one who loved those trips into town the most. It was another way to punish her further. Cherish would've rather been struck by her mother's hand than miss one of her favorite caramel flavored coffees that she got from the café at the farmers market.

She tiptoed down the stairs making sure to keep to the edges so the boards wouldn't creak. Finally, she reached the bottom and hurried over to the door. The two dogs were asleep on the floor of the living room and they jumped up as soon as she put her hand on the door. Wherever she was going, they wanted to go too.

With the two dogs following her, she made her way through the orchard. All she wanted to do was see what Florence was up to—catch a glimpse of her. Her big sister's life was exciting and she wanted to feel a part of that too.

When she got to the last row of trees, she couldn't see much, so then she decided to climb one of the trees.

"Ah, that's better." She'd gotten onto a branch about three feet off the ground, but that was all she needed to get a view of the cottage. Then she saw Carter's car. She watched the car pull up to the house and Florence got out followed by Carter.

It was hard getting used to seeing her in English clothes with her hair dancing about her shoulders, cut short like it was.

Had Florence set a path that she might follow?

It had never occurred to her to marry an *Englisher*. Now it had opened up a world of possibilities. She could see how suited Florence and Carter were to one another. With the world of English men opened up to her, the choices would be endless.

A smile met her lips. No longer would she confine her search for a husband within their Amish community. Even though she was too young to marry, that wouldn't stop her from looking. Besides that, she didn't think she was too young to date.

When Carter and Florence had shut their door, she

continued to stare at the cottage. Cherish used to feel sorry for Florence, the plain spinster version.

She'd been little more than a maid, cooking and sewing for the family, as well as looking after the orchard and running the store from the front of the property.

Florence had held all their lives together, and now Cherish could see things in the family, the household, and the orchard, beginning to erode.

Even though Florence had given them lessons about the orchard and apple growing, none of them was interested. No one took much notice because they always thought Florence would be around.

"Good for her, but not so good for us," Cherish said to herself as she stared at the house where her sister now lived. Since there was nothing to see, Cherish jumped down landing between Caramel, her dog, and Goldie, Joy's dog. "I'll race you back to the *haus*, guys." Cherish took off running and the dogs ran beside her.

Pretty soon she stopped running, but the dogs kept going. All she felt was despair. Her mother hated her, and worst of all, *Mamm* was getting married to Levi.

Was she supposed to call him *Dat?*

They couldn't make her.

She'd refuse.

After she got home, she poured herself a glass of milk and grabbed a handful of cookies before making her way upstairs.

She ate the cookies while writing a letter of instructions to her caretaker who was looking after the farm she'd inherited from Aunt Dagmar. He was a useless young man. The only good thing about him was that he was Aunt Dagmar's bishop's nephew. At least she had Ruth, the old lady from the neighboring farm, keeping an eye on him.

Even though she'd left a written account of what to do, the man seemed a bit simple. It wouldn't hurt to tell him again what needed to be done.

She brushed cookie crumbs off her letter and then a pain stabbed her heart. It wasn't because she'd just drunk a large glass of milk and eaten five cookies while barely chewing them. No, it was because the farm was calling.

How she longed to be out in the farm's air feeding the variety of animals, and making the baskets in front of the fire of an evening once all the work was done.

She had to get back there and look after the place. Otherwise, that caretaker would run it into the ground and all the hard work she and Aunt Dagmar had done would all be for naught.

Cherish let out a loud sigh.

That meant she'd have to behave if she wanted *Mamm* to allow her to return to the farm. They hadn't been getting along and that wouldn't be easy.

The other thing she could do was be so awful and uncontrollable that her mother wouldn't care where she went or what she did.

Two choices to consider.

Both ideas would work.

One easy and one hard.

What to do?

CHAPTER FOUR

*D*ays later, Florence was still finding her way around the new kitchen when she heard a buggy. In her heart, she hoped it was Wilma coming to connect with Carter, her first child, whom she had given to her older sister to raise. Florence gasped, suddenly struck by the thought that, technically, Wilma was her mother-in-law.

It was an awful thought.

Florence blinked hard and saw that it was not her stepmother, not even one of her half-sisters. It was her disagreeable sister-in-law, Christina.

Carter joined her in the kitchen. "Who is it?"

"It's Mark's wife, Christina. Funny that she's here without Mark. I haven't even heard from him since we've been back."

"You haven't told me much about her."

"There's not much to tell, really. I've never been able to get to know her very well." There wasn't much to tell him about Christina except that she was a miserable person, always sad and grouchy. Florence didn't want to say such negative things out loud; she felt bad for even thinking them. "I've got no idea why she's here. I hope everything's alright with the family."

"We'll soon find out."

"Come outside with me and meet her. She might not want to come into the house."

"Sure."

They walked out to meet her and she climbed down from the buggy, smiling. It was rare to see a smile on Christina's face.

Christina strode forward. "I'm so happy for you both." Then she stared at Carter. "I haven't met you before. You must be Carter." She held out both her hands and they shook hands awkwardly, with him placing a hand over the top of their clasped hands. Then they let go.

"Thank you for coming to visit us. Is everything alright with everyone?" Florence studied her sister-in-law's face. She didn't look like she was the bearer of bad news.

"Yes, as far as I know it is." Christina stood there smiling at both of them.

"Would you like to come inside?"

"Jah, I would."

That surprised Florence. Christina had never been

friendly toward her, and each time Florence had tried to get closer, Christina had seemed to push her away.

Once they were inside, Carter made his excuses. "I have work to do, so if you ladies will excuse me I'll just be upstairs."

"Sure, bye Carter." Christina smiled and he grinned back.

Carter headed up the stairs.

Christina took a look at her surroundings. "Mark said your family owned this place once."

"That's right. And *Dat* had to sell it a couple of years before he died. Carter bought it from the original people who bought it from *Dat.*"

"Interesting."

"It looks a bit different now that Carter's done some remodeling of the bathroom and ... he's had the entire kitchen redone. Come and take a look." She brought Christina into the kitchen and showed her all the 'mod cons' and electrical appliances.

"Well, you've really found a nice life for yourself, Florence." Christina sat down on one of the stools that were pushed up to the countertop.

"I'm happy." Florence giggled feeling she should share a little of her true feelings. "For the first time since *Dat* died, I can truly say I'm happy. Not just surface happy on the outside, but deep down."

"I'm glad."

"I'm quite surprised to see you. No one else has bothered to visit me. I didn't know if everybody would turn their backs on me. So … you and Mark are okay if I keep in contact?"

"Of course."

It was an unexpected response, but very much welcomed. "Good."

"I don't see why not."

"Can I fix you a hot cup of hot tea … or …?"

"That would be lovely, *denke.*"

As she made the tea, Christina watched everything she did. "Wilma's not too happy about you leaving suddenly, like you did."

Florence glanced over her shoulder at her sister-in-law. "I knew she wouldn't be pleased about it, but she's marrying Levi Brunner. She shouldn't waste her time thinking or talking about me." *Unless she's going to give me back the orchard.*

"I know. That will be a big change for her."

"And, I'm told, Levi will be running the orchard."

"I heard that. It must be hard for you to give up the orchard after all the work you put into it over the years, and your *vadder* before you."

Florence shook her head. *"Jah,* of course I had hoped things would be different."

"Sometimes, in life, things don't go the way we hoped."

"Often, it feels like, at least that's been my experience." Florence felt like there was an invisible barrier that had disappeared between Christina and herself. It seemed as though Christina wanted to be friends after all these years. "You seem a bit different now, Christina. Has anything changed in your life?" She secretly wondered whether Christina might have exciting baby news. It was the only reason she could think of for her to have such a personality shift.

"Everything's just the same as it always was." After a pause, she added, "Did you ever find out what Wilma did to me?"

CHAPTER FIVE

*F*lorence screwed up her face as she switched off the boiled kettle. She stared curiously at Christina, wondering what Wilma had done now. "No, what did she do?"

"As you probably know I met Mark when we are both on *rumspringa.*"

"Yes, I remember that, and you both came back to the community after *Dat* died and got married."

"Is that all you know?"

"Is there more?"

Christina nodded. "When I met Mark, I was pregnant with someone else's child."

"No!" Florence was shocked. "I had no idea. What became of the... Oh, you didn't lose the baby, did you?"

"Not in the way you're thinking. Of course, Mark knew

about the baby and it wasn't his and I wanted to keep the baby. Mark was fine with that decision and we were both willing to face the consequences of the community, whatever they would be."

This scenario was sounding familiar to Florence. This was what had happened to Wilma.

"Once Wilma found out about it, she encouraged me to give the baby up for adoption. When I say, 'encouraged,' I mean she forced me. She said if I gave the baby up I'd never regret it. She told me what happened to her and she said it was exactly the same and she knew she'd done the right thing."

"But, you obviously do regret it." Now things were falling into place. That explained Christina's constantly sour disposition. She was bitter with the nagging pain of regret.

"Of course, I do," Christina snapped. "Now I find out from Mark that Wilma told him that Carter's her child. And, she's rejecting him. Do you know what that tells me?"

"No, what?"

"It's obvious, Florence. She never wanted him in the first instance. I wanted my *boppli*, so what was she doing giving me advice?" Christina almost doubled over holding her stomach as though in physical pain. "I only gave the *boppli* away because I thought she knew best because she was older, do you see? I have carried unforgiveness in my heart toward Wilma ever since then, and even more so now, and I fear I always will."

Florence hesitated a moment piecing together all that Christina had said. Then she decided words weren't that important. She could see how her sister-in-law felt because it was written all over her pinched face. "I'm so sorry that you made the decision you regret, but can anyone truly be held at fault? The final decision was yours to make."

"I was in a vulnerable situation and I needed support from my family."

"What about Mark?"

"He said he'd go along with whatever decision I made. If we were to keep the child he would've raised it as his own. Wilma acted nice to me, she took me under her wing and explained all the consequences of each choice. The two main things she kept on about were the people in the community finding out, and the shame it would bring."

Florence nodded sympathetically. She could imagine Wilma saying that. She was always telling the girls they'd bring shame upon her.

"She said I would have many, many more with Mark and now I haven't got one single child. Not one! She said I'd have six in no time like she did, but I haven't."

"I'm sorry she said that and sorry you listened to her." Florence poured the hot water into the teapot, knowing now why Christina was so sour.

"The doctor said I can't have children. Or, if I did, it would be a one-in-a-million chance. I had that one-in-a-million chance, and Wilma ruined it. She said I needed to give the child away. She was a little girl."

Florence's eyes grew wide. "A baby girl …" That made it seem all the more real and she felt Christina's pain. After all, that child would've been raised as Florence's niece. Now she'd most likely never get to meet her.

"That's right. I'll never have a family, and Wilma took that from me."

"I'm so sorry to hear that, Christina."

"Do you know what it's like waiting and then watching people have *bopplis* so easily?"

"I felt a little bit of that watching all my friends and now some of my younger half-sisters getting married while thinking I had no hope of finding a man, so I can imagine that would be even worse for you."

"It is. Wilma should have kept her mouth closed."

"As much as I'm a little annoyed with Wilma right now, I don't think you can fully blame her. She didn't know you couldn't have any other children and she would've believed she was just trying to help you and advise you. Probably the way someone advised her many years ago. And she did keep your secret. I never knew about this."

Christina leaned forward. "She was very good at keeping secrets wasn't she. She kept her secret about Carter long enough."

"That's true, yes, she's very good at keeping secrets."

Florence licked her lips. "Have you ever thought about finding the child?"

"I can't do that, it might upset her and her family. I'll just have to wait and hope she comes to find me. That happens sometimes, you know."

"I know. I do hope she comes to find you. I'd love to meet her, too, when she does."

"If she does. Knowing my life, she won't. Nothing goes easily for me."

Florence poured out the tea into cups and then sat down with Christina to drink it. "Would you like something to eat with that? We've got chocolate chip cookies. Not home baked, but they're nice."

"Just the tea's fine, *denke.*"

Florence sat down next to Christina, and she brought the teacup to her lips and took a sip, then she placed the cup back gently on the saucer. "Thanks for telling me all that just now."

"I knew you'd understand now that you're not so close with Wilma."

"Have you heard when she's getting married?"

"Nee, I only heard about it the other day."

"Me too. It was a quite a shock I can tell you that. Although, I knew Levi liked her a lot, but I didn't think she returned his affections." She took another sip. "I guess I was wrong."

41

"She's just doing whatever suits herself. You've gone, and she needs someone around the place to do all the work."

Perhaps that summed up Wilma perfectly. "I have heard he's taking over the orchard. I was hoping to stay on and work the orchard and live here, but that's just not possible. I'm going to have a talk with her soon."

"Does she know that?"

Florence grimaced. "Not yet."

"Wilma's annoyed with you."

"With me?"

Christina nodded.

"For leaving?"

"Probably that too, but she's more upset you're opening an orchard in competition to hers." Christina slurped her hot tea.

That had been the last thing Florence had thought of. "I wonder how she heard that. It'll be years before we have any produce." It upset Florence to hear *her* orchard being referred to as Wilma's orchard. All Wilma had ever done was marry *Dat.* She'd never worked in it one day of her life—never showed the slightest bit of interest when anyone talked about the trees. She'd never plucked one apple from a tree, not even during harvest. Wilma always had an excuse when everyone was needed.

"Sorry. I shouldn't have said anything."

"Don't worry about it. And, ours won't be in competition.

There's more than enough business for everyone. Besides, it'll take years for us to get established."

"*Jah,* you said."

"Firstly, we have to work on the drainage, and then the soil and when the trees finally grow, it will be many more years before we can get enough apples to market. And more again before we can get our organic accreditation."

Christina's eyes glazed over. "I'm just telling you what she's been saying. She thinks you're out to ruin the orchard if you can't have control of it. Those are the very words she used. I know it sounds like I'm gossiping, but I'm not. You should know how she feels and know she's not going to be nice to you when you have that talk with her." She leaned forward and whispered, "She's already said she wants nothing to do with you and your husband."

"It's very sad that she thinks like that. I hope the girls don't believe I'd do anything of the kind. I only want the best for each one of them."

"Perhaps I shouldn't have said anything."

"No, I'm glad you did." She took another sip of tea. "If you don't mind me asking, why did the doctor say you couldn't have any children?"

"I had to have an operation when I was younger and I have a lot of internal scar tissue. There's that and also hormonal problems. They want to do a lot of medical treatments and operations, but I can't go through that. I told them no. I'm just hoping and praying for a miracle. That's what I do every single day and night."

"I'll help you pray."

She looked up from her tea and gave a weak smile. "Thank you, Florence, that's kind of you since you've left us."

"I'm the same person and I haven't left God." Christina simply stared at her and Florence didn't want to start a conversation that would most likely go nowhere except in circles. "Who else knows about Carter and Wilma—that Carter is Wilma's child?"

"No one apart from the family."

Florence nodded knowing that it would soon get out. The girls found it hard to keep information quiet and now Bliss would learn of it since Wilma would have to tell Levi Brunner, if she hadn't already.

"Come to dinner tomorrow night, you and Carter?"

Florence stared at her sister-in-law's smiling face. She seemed to be genuine in her friendship. "Oh, I'd love to. Would that be okay? I mean, Mark will still talk to me? He wasn't happy about my decision to marry Carter and he told me so when he came to Aunt Dagmar's funeral."

"What's done is done. He won't cast you aside."

Florence was relieved. She'd not yet gotten a letter back from Earl. She'd written her new cell phone number at the end of the letter, but he hadn't called either. The girls hadn't been in contact with her, so it looked like Mark and Christina were the only family members who were talking to her.

CHAPTER SIX

"*I*t's not the same without Florence here," Cherish announced at the breakfast table the next day as she sat with her three sisters and their mother.

"It's quieter, and more peaceful." *Mamm's* mouth turned down.

"It's not really quieter," Joy said. "She wasn't noisy and now there's one less person to help out around here."

"Will you stop talking about Florence?" *Mamm* glared at Joy and Cherish.

Favor said, "I think we're just all worried because nothing's been done with the orchard for several weeks."

"Exactly," Cherish said. "I wasn't going to say anything because no one listens to me, but we're in trouble. We need someone who knows what they're doing."

"Yeah," Hope agreed. "Florence was always doing something in the orchard every day and now no one is doing anything. So, it's not good."

"And that's what we live on," said Joy. "So … we were wondering. Who is running the orchard, *Mamm?"*

All eyes were on their mother.

Cherish said, "Didn't you say that Levi was taking it over?"

"Jah." Mama nodded. "I did say that, and he is."

Joy pressed her lips together. "Well he's not here doing anything."

"He'll be here by harvest time and when it's time to spray. He's got other things to do, you know. He can't be here every day. He said the orchard just needed workers to help at harvest time and then when it's time to spray. He's been getting advice."

"Florence would agree with that … *disagree* with that, I mean. She'd heartily disagree," Cherish said. "She was set against pesticides. We're an organic orchard. What's Levi thinking? He's obviously not thinking anything."

Joy shook her head. "This isn't good."

"Mamm, you're allowing *Dat's* orchard to slip away."

"What's going to become of us?" Cherish whimpered.

"Florence would be disappointed because … I mean, is it going to be organic spray?" Favor asked.

"You know it's not, Favor, so stop being silly. We have to

46

trust what Levi is doing. He'll be the new head of this household when we're married."

"He can be head of you. He won't be head of me," Cherish said to her mother. "I'll die before I let that happen."

"Cherish—"

"I'll not go to my room, *Mudder!*" Cherish glared at *Mamm.* "This is a serious thing. This is our livelihood we're talking about. He's not here working and it's worrying all of us."

"The point is, he's not doing anything, *Mamm,*" Joy said.

"He will be." She looked at the girls in turn. "Have you been talking about this amongst yourselves, then?"

"*Jah,* we have," Cherish said.

"You're all turning against me. This is all Florence's doing."

Hope said, "Because we're worried about what will become of us, and what will become of the orchard now that Florence is gone?"

Cherish nodded. "I'll say it because everyone is scared of how you'll react, but I'm not scared because I'm only saying the truth. We all have decided that we should get someone in to manage the place properly. Someone who knows what they're doing. Levi knows nothing about running an orchard."

"So, are all you girls against me now? If you are, you can go and live with Florence."

"I'd like to live anywhere but here," said Cherish.

"Everyone stop it," Joy shouted.

Cherish continued, "Everybody will be upset when the orchard is ruined just like that idiot is probably going to ruin my farm."

Mamm nodded. "That's another upset. The farm should've gone to all of you girls not just you, Cherish. If you weren't so selfish, you would've shared it with all of us. But you just ran off and signed those papers before you even told us she left the farm to you."

"I didn't give it a second thought. That was what Aunt Dagmar wanted."

Mamm frowned at her. *"Nee.* Surely Dagmar wasn't thinking clearly at the time she wrote that will. Her mind was affected."

"I won't share it with anybody because Dagmar and I were close. If she had wanted me to share it, she would've told me so. I'm not going to let anyone make me feel bad about it. That's the way things are. If you want to kick me out, I'll happily go back to the farm. I think that's where *Gott* wants me to go anyway."

"It's okay, Cherish. No one wants your farm. It's yours," Joy said. *"Mamm's* just upset."

"She should be," Cherish snapped back.

Mamm bounded to her feet and with an outstretched arm pointed to the door. "Go to your room now, Cherish."

"What have I done? I only spoke the truth."

"You better just go," Joy said. "*Mamm's* getting really upset."

"She's always getting upset these days. Maybe Levi has changed his mind about marrying her." When she saw the look of fury on *Mamm's* face, she scrambled to her feet and hurried out the door.

Then she continued her quick pace as she ran up the stairs.

Cherish didn't mean to say unkind things, but sometimes she just couldn't help it and she was just trying to make *Mamm* see that someone should be doing some kind of work in the orchard.

She was tired of missing Florence. It seemed silly not to go and see her since she only lived next door. *Mamm* had forbade them from talking to her, but Cherish seldom did what she was told. She knew Favor did anything she asked, and she didn't want to go there alone.

WHEN MID-AFTERNOON ARRIVED, like most afternoons, the Baker girls were in the midst of chores. Joy was in the kitchen cooking another dinner with which to impress Isaac, and Hope was in the kitchen, too, helping while talking to her.

Favor and Cherish had been given the job of sweeping and dusting, and then they were to clean the windows.

"Hey, Favor. Let's visit Florence."

Favor gasped. "We'd get into terrible trouble."

"Only if they find out. We won't be long."

Favor folded up her dusting rag. "What's the plan?"

"We spend a few more minutes in here and then we say we're cleaning the windows from outside. Then we run to her *haus*. It won't take too long. They need never know."

"Okay."

"Let's go now."

Favor giggled her okay. They put their rags down on the coffee table and set off.

"Where are you going?" Joy asked when the two girls walked through the kitchen, heading to the back doorway from the laundry room, on their way outside.

Favor said, "All the smudges on the windows are on the outside."

"Jah," Cherish agreed. "We're going to clean the outside first."

"Good idea," Hope said as she chopped the carrots.

"After you finish your chores, we need some apples peeled. Don't forget we're making apple pies."

"We won't forget," Cherish said as she pushed Favor through the door.

Once they were outside, they both ran as fast as they could through the trees. When they came to the last tree, they saw Florence and Carter's cottage.

CHAPTER SEVEN

"That didn't take long." They slowed their pace, and slipped through the barbed wire fence that separated the properties.

FLORENCE WAS SITTING in the living room planning out the next few months of preparing the ground for the trees, when movement outside the window caught her attention. She was overjoyed to see her two youngest sisters hurrying to the house.

When she got off the couch, Spot woke up and then followed her to the front door. He sat beside her when she opened the door and they watched the girls make their way to the house together.

The girls ran up the steps and then the three hugged each other at the same time.

"What are you doing here?" She looked at both of their flushed faces. "Does *Mamm* know you're here?"

"Nee," Favor said.

"She's asleep."

"You've got a dog?" Favor asked.

"Yeah, it's Carter's dog, Spot. I guess he's my dog now, too." Both girls patted the dog while he lowered his head. "He's a little shy sometimes. Come inside."

"Is Carter here?" asked Cherish.

"He's in town."

As they walked into the house, Cherish asked, "So, you really married him?"

"I did. Come into the kitchen. Would you like milk and cookies?"

"Jah," both girls chorused.

When the girls were seated, they talked about how much the cottage had changed.

"It looks nothing like I remembered."

"Me either," said Favor. "I thought the ceilings were higher."

"They're normal height. You were a lot smaller when you were here last."

"That must be it."

Florence poured out two glasses of milk and set a plate of cookies in front of them.

"I have trees back home and they don't belong to the orchard. Do you remember *Dat's* special trees that he collected?"

"I do," said Favor. "They're at the side of the *haus.*"

"That's right. Do you think it would be all right with *Mamm* if I had them?"

Cherish frowned. "You want her to give them to you?"

"Yes. Well, one is mine already. Carter gave it to me."

Favor shook her head. "I dunno. She said the ones that don't bear fruit she's burning. I knew she meant *Dat's* special ones."

"There's the one Carter gave me, she can't do anything with that one, surely."

"She can if you left it there." Cherish bit into a cookie.

Florence reminded herself that they were just trees, special trees, but what could she do if Wilma refused to give them to her? She just hoped Wilma wouldn't destroy them.

"When is *Mamm* marrying Levi?"

"We don't know yet."

"He's taken over the orchard already. She's shown him the books and he said he's learning what to do. He said he doesn't agree with the organic idea and the place would make more money without it."

"I knew it," Florence blurted out. That had been what their whole focus and business plan was based on. "Without being organic we won't be able to compete with the cheaper imported apples. I mean, *you* won't be able to. They're sold on price not the quality of the taste or the health benefits. That's so upsetting."

"It's true." Cherish took another cookie before she'd finished the first.

"But all our customers are waiting each year for our produce. Ah, um … your produce."

"Just tellin' you what I heard them talking about," Cherish said. "I said to him to leave things how they are and *Mamm* sent me to my room for being rude." Cherish shook her head. "He's not my *vadder.* I hope he doesn't think he can tell me what to do when he marries *Mamm.* I'll run away. I'll go back to my farm."

"Nee, don't do that and leave me alone. Joy'll marry soon and it'll be just me and Hope."

"Where is Hope?"

"Home."

"She didn't want to see me?"

"She's cooking with Joy and we're supposed to be cleaning the outsides of the windows."

"Why's that?"

Before Favor could answer, a realization dawned on Florence. "I just realized. I'll never get organic accreditation if my neighbors are spraying so closely."

"Surely that's not right if you're not."

"Well, the soil has to be tested and it's not likely. The spray will come this way."

"There must be a solution," said Favor.

"There isn't one. Not unless Levi decides not to spray."

"We'll try to make him see sense."

Cherish shook her head. "Why would he listen to us?"

"We'll have to try."

"Yes, please try."

"Mamm's upset with you," Favor said.

"I knew she would be. I've brought shame upon her and the family and I am opening a competing orchard, and probably many other things."

"We'll have to get back soon before they see we're missing." Cherish reached for her third cookie.

"How's everything at your farm, Cherish?"

"I'm trying not to think about it. I'm sure the new caretaker will run it into the ground. I only hope I've got something to take over when I'm old enough."

"At least you have a plan," Favor said. "I have nothing to think about."

"Come with me to the farm when I go and we'll live together."

"Jah denke, Cherish. I might."

Cherish got off the stool. "We really have to leave. Mind if I have another cookie?"

"Sure. Take as many as you want."

Cherish grabbed hold of two more. "Two's enough."

"I'll take another, too," said Favor.

When both girls had taken cookies, they said their good-byes, and then headed out the door. With Spot curled up asleep on the couch, Florence watched the girls walk away.

At least they were still talking to her even if they had to sneak away to do it.

CHAPTER EIGHT

As Florence and Carter drove the short distance to Mark and Christina's house to have a meal with them, Florence thought about the mother that she and Mark shared. "I just thought … since my mother was an *Englisher,* there's a good chance there might be a photo of her out there somewhere."

"I'd say so. It's more than likely. What was her maiden name?"

"I don't know. If I did know, I've forgotten. It would be in the boxes in the attic on some paperwork. Only thing is, Wilma might not want me to have her things."

"Surely she'd give them to you if you ask?"

"I'll write a note. I can't face her, not after the way I left."

"Okay. Good idea. When you're ready I'll contact the man, who helped me to find Wilma."

"Thanks."

"Maybe Mark will know her maiden name."

"I hope so. Tonight'll be the night to find out."

It was a relief for Florence to see her brother's smiling face when he opened the door of his house with Christina by his side. He reached forward and gave her a hug, something that he rarely did. Then he shook Carter's hand. "I'm pleased to meet you," he said as Christina introduced them.

"You both took us all by surprise." Mark backed away so they could enter into the house.

"It was brewing for a while," Carter said, smiling.

"Come through to the kitchen. Dinner's two minutes away from being served."

"It smells delicious," Carter said.

"It's a roast. It's Mark's favorite, and I think most men like roast. How about you, Carter?"

"I like a roast too. That's perfect."

"Carter's not used to home-cooked food yet. He's easily satisfied. Oh, I didn't mean that the way it sounded. I know it'll be perfectly delicious especially since Carter used to eat different—"

"A lot of take-out meals. That's what Florence means."

"That's right."

"Florence is a great cook too," Mark told Carter.

"I know. I'm a lucky man. Um, fortunate ... blessed."

Christina laughed. "You don't have to watch what you say around us, Carter."

Carter chuckled. "Good to know."

Florence could tell Carter was nervous. This was the first time she'd seen him like that.

The three of them sat down while Christina placed bowls of cooked vegetables in front of them. Lastly, the already sliced roast was set onto the table. They all closed their eyes for the silent prayer.

Florence had forewarned him about the silent prayer that was said by each individual before every meal. She still prayed before she ate at home and now Carter was used to that.

When all eyes were open, Christina stood and served the meat onto each plate and then left everyone to serve themselves from the dishes of mashed potatoes, greens, and turnips.

Florence said, "Mark, did you know our mother was raised as an *Englisher?*"

He stopped chewing, opened his eyes wide and stared at her. "I didn't know. Are you certain?"

She nodded. "I found that out. Remember how I came to see you awhile ago at your store and I mentioned how no one ever talks about her and I was trying to find out why?"

"I remember you being curious about her, but why dredge up the past?"

Florence was a little shocked. She had hoped he'd help her locate the rest of their extended family. "I want to know more about her."

"It's only reasonable that Florence is curious about her own mother, her mother who gave birth to her." Christina stared at Mark. "Aren't you curious, too?"

He shook his head. "My earthly parents have both died and I don't see why there's any point in finding out about them. We are who we are and nothing will change that." When Florence didn't say anything, he added, "If you find out about her, what will change in your life?"

"I don't know." She bit her lip. "I guess I just miss her. I don't remember as much as you do. I remember a couple of hazy vague things about her and that's all."

Christina asked, "What do you remember, Mark?"

"I don't remember much about her either."

"I just want to know what she looked like and I figured if she has some relatives out there, they might have a photo and then I'll be able to see her."

Christina said, "Maybe Wilma was always so horrible to you because she was jealous of your mother."

Mark shot Christina a look and then she looked down at her food.

Florence felt she had to set Christina right. Wilma hadn't always been horrible. "It can't have been easy having three step children and being the second wife. She did a good job—the best she could, I'm sure."

"If you feel that way about Wilma, why do you want to find out more about our mother?"

"I just miss her and want to feel closer to her."

"I don't understand it." Mark cut a portion of meat and popped it into his mouth.

Carter and Florence looked at each other and then he asked Mark, "Do you remember her maiden name?"

Mark swallowed his mouthful. "I don't remember it ever being mentioned. Maybe Ada will know something. Have you talked to her? Or perhaps Earl?"

She didn't even know if Earl was talking to her. Perhaps he didn't ever get her letter. Enough time had passed for him to get the letter and to reply, or at least to call the new cell phone that Carter had insisted she keep. She'd added the number to the letter. "No, I haven't. That's a good idea. I'll write to him and … I don't know if Ada will want to see me."

"Perhaps you can ask Ada for her," Christina said to Mark.

"*Nee.* I want to be left out of it." He looked over at Florence. "You should leave things be, too."

She saw his worried face and gave him a smile before changing the subject. "And how are *Mamm* and the girls?" She couldn't tell him about Favor and Cherish's visit; they'd get into trouble if *Mamm* found out.

"Just the same as ever. It'll be a big change when she marries Levi. That was a big surprise to everybody."

"Not to me. I knew he liked her a lot, but I always thought

she wasn't that interested. He's taking over running the orchard, did you hear that?" Florence was doing her best not to let the whole thing upset her, but it was hard.

"Does he know anything about orchards, Florence?" asked Christina.

Mark spoke before Florence had a chance. "It won't take him long to learn."

Her brother's comment annoyed Florence. It had taken her father years to gather his knowledge and he taught Florence everything. To say it wouldn't take long felt dismissive; like he thought her knowledge was of no consequence. "I'm sorry, Mark, but I disagree." She went on to explain the problem regarding the spraying and the impact it would have on the surrounding properties.

"I didn't know. I agree. It's better to keep going in the direction *Dat* set. I'll make a special visit tomorrow and talk to Wilma."

"Would you?"

He nodded. *"Jah.* I'll do my best. I'll leave Isaac as soon as we open the doors. It's our least busy time. Isaac can do without me for an hour or so."

"That's wonderful. I hope you have some success."

"Me too. I'll do my best. The whole community needs to work together, and not just our Amish community, the broader community."

CHAPTER NINE

$\mathscr{D}$ays later after Florence had gotten some guidance from one of her father's old friends, she sat down to plan how her orchard should take shape. She was more than a little sad when she found out how long the whole process would take.

Now that she wasn't bound by the rules of the Amish bishop and the *Ordnung,* she could use machinery to prepare the soil and dig the trenches for the drainage. When they worked out exactly what needed to be done, it could all be done in no time.

She smiled at the thought of doing things speedily.

"Warning," Carter called out from his upstairs office.

"What do you mean?" Florence called back.

"Wilma's driving toward us."

Florence jumped up and looked out the front door. Wilma's buggy was nearly at the house.

Carter appeared by her side. "I wonder what she wants."

Florence glanced at him. "Maybe she wants to get to know you better."

"I doubt it. Wouldn't Mark have seen her by now?"

"That's right. I was so busy thinking about planning the orchard that I clean forgot about that."

When Wilma pulled up the buggy, they both walked to meet her.

She got out of the buggy and ignored Carter completely, staring straight at Florence. "I can't believe what you're doing. I hear from Eric Brosley that you're starting an orchard here."

"I am. Are you going to say hello?"

"Hello." She glanced at Carter and gave a curt nod, then turned her attention back to Florence. "The land's not good, that's why *Dat* sold it off."

"Oh, well, I've got information on how to make it better. Don't worry about us."

"Why are you doing this to us?"

"Florence is doing nothing to you," Carter said.

At the same moment, Florence asked, "What am I doing?"

"You're in opposition to us."

Wilma had it all wrong, but right now Florence was worried about something more important. "Levi knows he can't spray, right?"

"He said spraying is the only way. He doesn't go along with your—"

"What?" Florence cried. "Tell him no. He can't."

"I'm just telling you what he said. Levi has studied what to do. He said it's not as hard as everyone says."

"Do you know the damage that one orchard spraying will do to its neighbors who have organic fruit? There's a good chance they'll be contaminated and won't pass the regular testing."

"Modernize things. That's what it will do. Levi and I have decided."

"It's not modernizing. It's going backward. He's ruining it for me and for the Jenkins. Mr. Jenkins has cherries as well as apples, all grown organically. If Levi goes ahead it'll be disastrous."

Carter cleared his throat. "I've been meaning to talk to you about that, Florence. It was going to be a surprise."

Florence stared at Carter. Now wasn't the time to surprise her with anything. Not in front of Wilma. "What was?"

"I was going to take you there later today. We now own the Jenkins farm. They're running it for us."

Florence was shocked. He'd bought up the two plots of land leading away from her old orchard, and now he'd bought the orchard on the other side of Wilma?

Wilma's face immediately soured. "You think that's the answer—throwing money around? I heard you'd bought up all the land around here. We're not for sale, just in case you try to buy us out next. Florence, what good is it if you gain the whole world and lose your own soul?"

"We never asked to buy it," said Carter. "They approached me."

Florence was upset with Wilma. "We're not trying to gain the whole world and no one has lost their soul."

"I've studied many religions and the overriding message is love and forgiveness. I figure if I show that, I'll be right—we'll be all right." Carter smiled at his birth mother, but she would barely look at him.

Florence was pleased Carter was defending himself, but it was no use speaking to people whose hearts were hardened in their ways.

"There's more to it than that," Wilma hissed. "Haven't you told him anything, Florence?"

"It's not for you to concern yourself with, Wilma. Now, about the orchard. I was going to come and see you to ask if you'd consider … I'd like to come over and get the heritage trees *Dat* collected. They aren't part of the orchard and hardly produce much fruit anyway."

"*Nee.* When you left, you left with everything you deserved. You won't come and take anything away from me and my girls."

Wilma's words no longer hurt her—she wouldn't let them. She had Carter now and that was all that mattered. Before she asked for her special tree, she thought she'd soften it by talking about something that made Wilma happy. "When are you marrying Levi?"

"Soon, and you're not invited."

"I didn't think I would be."

"Then you won't be disappointed."

"No, I'm not! I have a tree there that Carter gave me. I need that one back at the very least."

Wilma tugged on the strings of her *kapp*. "I don't know which one it is and I don't want you coming around there."

"It has a pink tag on the top branch. It's only small."

Wilma nodded. "I'll see if I can find it and if I can, I'll bring it by."

"Thank you. Also, how is Levi finding out what he should be doing with the orchard?" What she meant was, why had he chosen to spray? He had to be getting bad advice from somewhere.

"I don't know." Wilma abruptly stared at Carter. "Is this the way you take revenge on me; taking Florence away from us so we'd all fall apart?"

"Who's falling apart?" Florence snapped back. "I'm not."

"I'm in love with Florence. It was her own decision to marry me and we're happy. It had nothing to do with you. If you're falling apart, it has to do with you, not me or Florence."

"Rubbish! You knew from the very beginning that you were buying the place that …"

"Stop it, Wilma."

"Oh, it's Wilma now, is it?"

"The way you're behaving to me, you don't deserve to be called *Mamm.*" Florence figured she'd gone that far, she might as well keep going. "Please leave my property."

Carter put his hand on Florence's arm. Wilma turned away and got back into her buggy. They stood there and watched her drive away.

"I shouldn't have done that. I'll have to wait until things cool down and apologize."

"I never knew you had a temper."

She faced him. "I don't."

"Hmm, good to know."

"It's just that sometimes things slip out of my mouth before I have a chance to stop them."

"I'll remember that."

"Now, about the Jenkins' orchard?"

"Like I said, they approached me when they heard I'd bought the neighboring properties. They wanted out, they'd been talking privately about selling, so I bought it."

"Oh."

"It was a good business decision. That's all. It made sense."

"Also makes a lot of work when it's just the two of us."

"We better hurry up and make that family, then."

She giggled. "But seriously, do you see what I mean?"

"We'll pay workers when the Jenkins leave. I negotiated that they stay on for one year. They've agreed to run it and we've negotiated wages. I'm sorry I didn't tell you sooner. I was going to surprise you later today."

"It sure was a surprise. I need to know everything from now on. This isn't the first thing you've kept from me."

"I'll make sure it's the last." He drew her into his arms.

"Good. Are you upset by how Wilma is acting?"

"I had hoped for a different reunion, but I had been warned by Iris that she'd want nothing to do with me. I wasn't surprised, but truthfully, I couldn't help being a little disappointed."

She nodded. "I can understand that."

She put her head on his shoulder.

THAT AFTERNOON, he took her to see the Jenkins' orchard. They were *Englishers.* Mr. Jenkins gave them a tour and when they were done, they sat and had lemonade and carrot cake with Mrs. Jenkins and their teenage son, Fairfax. Fairfax was upset that his parents had sold to retire. He'd wanted to take over, but he was still too young. They'd had him late in life. Florence felt sorry for him—

SAMANTHA PRICE

he reminded her a little of Cherish and her inherited farm
—and she intended to speak to Carter about keeping
Fairfax on as a worker if he proved helpful over the next
year.

CHAPTER TEN

The next morning, Florence felt out of sorts. She'd not slept for worrying about Wilma and how she'd sent her away. When Carter left for an appointment to sort out something with the bank, Florence decided to walk to her old family house and put a note on the doorstep. She'd apologize to Wilma and also ask for her mother's things. Wilma would have no use for them and she didn't want them to be thrown out. There was also no point talking to Wilma face-to-face, she figured. They'd only have another argument.

Florence hoped no one would see her. She went the long way around the barn so she wouldn't be seen from the kitchen window. Just when she stepped onto the porch, the front door opened.

It was Joy.

They stared at each other for a moment before Joy spoke.

"What are you doing here after the way you treated *Mamm?*"

Florence walked forward and handed her the note. "This is a letter of apology."

She took it from her and closed her hands around it. "She's not home."

"Oh. Then, will you give it to her?"

"Of course."

"Thank you."

"It's good to see you, Florence."

"You too."

Joy stepped forward and hugged her. They'd always gotten along well and Florence was pleased Joy hadn't hardened her heart against her.

When they finished their embrace, Florence said, "In the note, I asked if I can collect my mother's things. They're in the attic."

"I'm sure that's all right. Do you want them now?"

"Um, I think it best ..."

"Of course. Ask *Mamm* first. Good idea. I'll give her the note. I'll make certain she'll say yes. It's only right that you have your *mudder's* things."

"*Denke*, Joy. I hope she sees it that way."

"Don't worry, she will."

"There are quite a few boxes."

"It's okay. I'll have Isaac bring them to you in his buggy."

"Would you?"

"*Jah*, of course."

"Thank you." Florence wanted to get away before Wilma got home. "It's nice to see you, Joy." She gave Joy a brief hug and then stepped back.

"You too."

Florence hurried away from the house wondering why she didn't get an earful of Scriptures from Joy about leaving the community. Did Joy think she was a lost soul, beyond all hope and redemption?

MEANWHILE, the bishop had caught up with Cherish and he'd arranged a meeting with the elders. Wilma drove her.

There were two elders, sitting one at either side of the bishop in his living room, and she sat opposite while her mother and the bishop's wife were in the kitchen.

"Did you think I'd forget, Cherish?" the bishop asked.

"Forget?"

"*Jah*, forget that you were seen with Tom in the early hours of the morning."

Her heart beat increased, but she was determined not to let her face show that she was scared. It was awful talking to the bishop. It was like he could see into her mind and was judging her for all her wicked thoughts. "Well, he told you what happened, didn't he?"

"What do *you* say happened?" one of the elders asked. "Never mind what he said."

"It's so hard because it happened so long ago. I couldn't sleep, I went walking and pretty soon I was far from home. Fortunately for me, Tom gave me a ride home."

"And what was Tom doing out so late?"

"I assumed he was on his way to work. Wasn't he?"

None of them looked pleased with her remark.

"It was only a little past midnight," the bishop said after the man to his right whispered in his ear.

"I'm not sure." Cherish shook her head. "You'll have to ask him."

The bishop said, "We've already talked to him."

"Look, I've done nothing wrong and neither has Tom, as far as I know. There's really nothing to worry about. Now, can I go?"

"Nee. We don't think you're telling us the truth, but *Gott* knows. He sees everything."

"Jah, He does. Truly, I've done nothing wrong."

"Did you both arrange to meet one another?"

Cherish found herself getting bored with all the back and forth. When she was younger, she would've been more scared, but now she knew she could leave the Amish community behind her just like Florence had. The bishop and his elders held no power in the outside world. "All right, we did."

The bishop and the elders looked at one another. The truth was clearly an answer they weren't expecting.

"You were aware he was engaged to be married to Isabel at the time?"

"I can't remember all the details of who was betrothed to whom, dating, engaged or what not. It was so long ago." Cherish felt bad for blurting out the truth when Tom must've glossed over it. Now, he'd get into trouble. She hadn't wanted for that to happen.

"The other thing that's a concern here is your age. That's the most concerning," the bishop said as he glared at Cherish. "Let's start at the beginning. Whose idea was it? Your's or Tom's?"

"I'm sorry. I don't remember the details. I keep saying that. Can I go home now?"

"You must remember if he asked you to leave the house in the middle of the night. Did *you* ask him to meet you?"

"I can't say more."

The bishop leaned forward. "Can't or won't?"

"Does it matter?" The more she talked back, the more she felt empowered.

"Can you go to the kitchen and send your *mudder* in here please?"

"Okay." Cherish walked to the kitchen feeling a little sorry for Wilma. It was up to the parents to discipline their children and right now, she knew the elders were thinking Wilma had done a terrible job. Cherish wondered if they had any idea how much of that *Mamm* had left to Florence after *Dat's* death...

"Mamm, they want to talk with you."

Wilma smirked, and walked past her without saying anything. Cherish stayed in the kitchen for ten minutes before her mother walked in.

"We're going home."

Wilma wasn't smirking now. They walked out of the house and got into the buggy.

"What happened, *Mamm?"* Cherish asked when the buggy was halfway down the driveway.

"They're blaming me for your actions."

"I'm sorry, but better that than blaming me." Cherish laughed, but stopped when her mother looked at her with eyes blazing. "Sorry, *Mamm."*

"You will be. I'll make sure of that. I'll figure out a fitting punishment for you when we get home."

"You could send me off to the farm. I'm old enough to live alone. I'll be happy there without people around. I liked it when you sent me away."

"You can go to hell for all I care. How dare you embarrass me like this? I don't want you anywhere near me."

Cherish was shocked and didn't say anything further. They sat in silence all the way home.

When they finally arrived home, Joy met them as they got out of the buggy. She was in tears, and she delivered some dreadful news.

CHAPTER ELEVEN

*T*he very next morning, as Carter rinsed out his coffee mug, he looked out the window.

"What is it?" Florence asked wondering if the cows were doing something odd. He couldn't have been looking at Spot because he was still inside.

"It's one of your bonnet sisters."

"They're actually your half-sisters, too. Just as much as they are mine, which is kind of weird. Who is it?"

"No idea which one it is. Can't see from this distance. I can see she's crying."

"Oh no. I'm guessing it'll be Cherish. She'd be the one most likely to come to me in the middle of some kind of disaster."

"Cherish—the troublemaker?"

"Yes." Florence stood up and walked over to the window.

It *was* Cherish and she was clearly distressed. She turned to Carter. "It must be an emergency." Florence spun on her heel and hurried to the front door wondering who had died.

When Cherish got closer, Florence saw her tear-stained face and her heart went out to her. Rarely did Cherish cry about anything. She was the type of girl who didn't let anything get to her. Florence hurried down the steps and ran to her. "What's the matter?"

Cherish drew in a couple of deep breaths as though she were gasping for air.

"Talk to me, Cherish. What's wrong?"

"It's Mercy." She took another breath. "She's lost the baby."

Florence felt like all the wind had been knocked out of her. "Oh no." Everyone had been so excited about the first grandchild for Wilma, and the first of the new generation.

"It happened five days ago and we're just finding out about it now. She was too upset to talk to us, she said."

"Oh, that's terrible."

Cherish collapsed into Florence's arms. Florence glanced back at the house and saw Carter staring at them with his arms folded. She knew he was frustrated, but what was she to do? The girls still needed her and she couldn't turn her back on them. "I suppose she's taking it really badly?"

"She is. She's coming here to get away, coming to have a little break. She wants to see you."

"Me?"

"*Jah.* We spoke to her last night on the phone and that's when she said she wants to see you."

"I'm pleased she's getting away to clear her head, but seeing me will cause trouble. *Mamm's* not happy with me already, I know that much. She'll say I'm a bad influence."

"Mercy doesn't care what *Mamm* or Ada says. She already said that. She said you'll always be part of our family."

Now she knew for certain that Ada, *Mamm's* best friend, was upset with her as well, but that was only to be expected. At least now it was spelled out. "How's *Mamm* taking the news?"

"She went up to her room and hasn't come out yet. You know what? I think you should come and talk to her."

"Me? No, I couldn't."

"*Mamm* needs someone to talk with, and you always had a way of calming her down whenever she was upset about anything."

"Things have changed. She's dreadfully upset with me and with Carter."

"What did you do other than leave the community?"

"It's over the orchard as well as me leaving, I think. It's best I stay away and I know that for sure. She won't be happy to see me."

"It's just not right without you there." Cherish shook her head.

"I know, but you'll have to get used to it because I'm not coming back."

Cherish pouted as she looked over toward the house, at Carter who was now leaning against the doorway at the front of the house. "I hope he's worth it."

"He is. I made the right decision. I'm happy now — happier than I've ever been."

"That's fine for you, but what about us?"

Florence smiled. Cherish hadn't changed. "Do you want to come inside?"

"Okay. Do you have more cookies?"

"We do."

Once they were inside, Carter made his excuses and went upstairs to do some office work.

"How is everyone?" Florence asked, as she switched on the electric teakettle.

"Dreadful, now. I don't think Mercy will ever get over it."

"Maybe not. Tea or coffee?"

"Tea, just black and weak." Cherish leaned forward and whispered, "Are you going to have babies, Florence? Babies with that man?"

"That man has a name, and he's your half-brother, and his name is Carter."

"Oh, I wasn't being disrespectful. I know you love him

very much and that's fine. I'm just sad for myself that you left."

Florence spooned loose-leaf tea into the waiting teapot. "Any news from the farm?"

"Farm?"

"Yes, Aunt Dagmar's farm?"

Cherish sighed. "He never answers the phone when I call. Do you think he knows it's me calling?"

Florence tried hard to keep from smiling. She knew that the 'he' to whom her sister was referring was the caretaker she'd left in control of the farm. Cherish didn't see eye-to-eye with him, but for Cherish that wasn't unusual. "Maybe the phone lines are out of order?"

"Nee, I called Bishop Zachariah and he said they're fine. The phone in his barn is working and so the phone in my barn should be, too. I don't know, maybe he has a hearing problem and just can't hear it."

"Could be, or maybe he's very busy when you call. The farm's a lot of work. When was the last time you heard from Malachi?"

Cherish pouted. "I don't know. Would you come back there with me one time and visit?"

Florence knew that Carter would hate her being involved that far. Not only that, *Mamm* would forbid it.

"I don't think people would be happy about that."

"If you're talking about *Mamm,* she said she doesn't care

about me anymore, or what I do. She said I could go to hell for all she cared."

Florence gasped "Really?"

"Jah, she's mad at me."

Right then, Florence was flooded with guilt for leaving. Things were falling apart fast without her. And, if things with the family were this bad, what was to come of her beloved orchard? "Why's she mad at you? What did you do?"

"Not much really. She's upset ever since I had to go and talk with the bishop. She was supposed to punish me but so far she hasn't."

Florence had clean forgotten about the trouble Cherish had gotten into when she had been seen with a man who was engaged. Not only that, it was in the very-early hours of the morning, and the two of them were seen alone. Cherish had been all set to meet with the bishop and the elders regarding it, but she'd had to suddenly go to Aunt Dagmar's to look after her. "Is that about you being seen with Tom, or is it about something else?"

"When I got back, nothing was said to me. So, of course, I wasn't going to remind the bishop. That would've been stupid."

"So why ..." Florence's head started spinning while Cherish was talking. It reminded her of all the pressure she used to have before she'd escaped the family to be with Carter.

"I had nothing to do with Tom canceling his engagement."

Now the pieces were coming together. "What? Do you mean Isabel and Tom aren't getting married now?"

"That's right. And it has nothing to do with me. I've only seen Tom a few times since then."

Florence found it hard to believe Cherish. "Tom is so much older than you are."

"Exactly and I don't even like him, not like that. I think I sort of did, back then."

"Does Tom know it?" The teakettle whistled and Florence got up to fix the hot tea.

"I don't know. How can I know what someone knows?"

Florence glanced over at Cherish. Her youngest sister had always been one to handle the truth loosely. "Is that why he broke off his engagement?"

They were interrupted by Carter clearing his throat loudly in the upstairs room.

They both looked upward.

"Noise certainly travels in this *haus*," Cherish whispered.

"It does; I think we have to keep our voices down." Florence figured the tea had sat long enough to steep, so she poured out two cups and handed one to Cherish. Then Florence sat down next to Cherish once more. She lowered her voice to save Carter from the aggravation of the family dramas that had been Florence's life for so long. "Did it ever occur to you that Tom might've broken off his engagement with Isabel because he thought he could marry you?"

"Nee." Cherish took a sip of tea and avoided looking at Florence.

Cherish was too attractive for her own good and it could very well lead her into trouble in the future, if it hadn't already. Florence knew she and *Mamm* had made the right decision back when they'd banished Cherish to Aunt Dagmar's, but now that Cherish was getting older it was getting harder to protect her. Florence understood that it was no longer her own responsibility, but she still loved her sister and it was clear *Mamm* was not stepping up to accept the challenge.

"Anyway, Mercy's coming home. She said she's going to see you."

"Oh. What would *Mamm* think about that?"

"I don't know, but Mercy needs you."

CHAPTER TWELVE

*A*fter Cherish left, Florence and Carter had their first disagreement.

He didn't like her associating with her 'bonnet sisters' as he called them. He told her they were pulling her down when she should be free of them.

How could she turn her back on them? Especially now that Mercy had miscarried.

He drew his dark eyebrows together. "They're all ungrateful leeches, who are still trying to suck the life out of you even though you've gotten away."

"They're not."

"We should move away. Far away from them."

"No, we're okay here."

She could see Carter was doing his best not to be impatient with her, but she couldn't turn her back on her family. She still wanted the best for the girls and if they needed her help, she always wanted to be there to give it.

I T WAS two days after Cherish's visit, just after eleven in the morning when Florence glanced out the window for the umpteenth time that day. She wasn't sure what day Mercy was coming, but with Carter having a meeting in town, she hoped it would be today.

Then she saw two figures heading toward the fence. She was so pleased to see them. Now Mercy and Cherish were doing their best to help each other get through the barbed wire fence while not snagging their long dresses.

Spot had been sleeping on the couch, but raised his head when he sensed someone. He jumped off the couch and went to the door and scratched it. Florence moved to the door and opened it. "These are my sisters, Spot."

Spot looked over at them, had a good stare and then went back to the couch. He showed about as much interest in them as Carter did.

Florence stepped out of the house and waited on the porch for them. Mercy lifted her hand and waved. Florence waved back noticing that there was no smile on Mercy's lips, which was totally understandable.

Mercy walked up the porch steps first followed closely by Cherish. Florence held out her arms and Mercy walked into them and sobbed on Florence's shoulder. "I feel so bad, Florence."

"I know you do. I'm so sorry about your *boppli.*"

"*Denke.*"

After the longest embrace, Florence said, "Come inside." They walked in, and she sat the girls down on the couch. "I'll make us a pot of nice hot tea."

"You stay there and talk to her, Florence. I'll get the tea."

"Is Carter home?" Mercy asked.

"No, he had to go to a meeting today."

Mercy nodded and looked around. "I would've loved to meet him and see what he's like."

"That's Spot," Florence told Mercy when her gaze had settled on the dog as he closed his eyes.

"Nice dog."

"Thanks." She thought she had to make an excuse for the dog not being friendly. "He sleeps most of the day."

"Are you happy, Florence?"

"I'm happier than I've ever been."

"I wish I could say the same. I've never felt so much sadness. Not even when *Dat* died."

Tears stung behind Florence's eyes. She could only imagine how devastated both Mercy and Stephen were.

"I had everything planned. I had names and everything. One for a boy and one for a girl. We painted the room, Stephen and his *vadder* made the crib and now there's no *boppli.* All I feel is emptiness. There's a hole where my heart used to be."

Florence bit into a fingernail. There was no appropriate thing to say. Nothing to take away her sister's pain.

Mercy added, "The bishop's wife said Jesus wanted the *boppli* with Him. What do you think, Florence? Why couldn't I have had my *boppli?* It's only right."

"I don't have any answers. I believe Jesus is taking care of the baby for you, but I don't think He deliberately took the baby away from you. I wish there was something I could say or do to make you feel better."

"Just seeing you helps. I told Stephen I wanted to move home and he said we could if I wanted to. He said he'd find work here somewhere, but now that I have gotten back home, I don't want to move back here. Nothing's the same as it was. *Mamm's* about to marry Levi Brunner and with you gone ... things have changed. I prefer to stay where we are."

Florence didn't know what to say. She could hear a lot of clattering sounds from the kitchen and hoped Cherish was not breaking anything. If she broke anything in Carter's beloved kitchen it would add fuel to his fire of contempt for the bonnet sisters and their continual dramas.

"Has *Mamm* spoken to you since you left?" Mercy asked.

"We haven't spoken much, not really. Just about the orchard and it wasn't a pleasant conversation. We have different ... differing views on how the orchard should be managed, but I've got no say in that anymore."

"I heard a little about that. Cherish told me." Mercy paused for a moment. "They don't know why I lost it. They said it sometimes happens, but I'm just worried if something like that might happen next time."

"I can understand why you would be concerned." Florence nodded.

"Do you?"

"Yes, of course. It's natural to be fearful about something like that."

"Joy tells me I shouldn't be fearful. She said—"

"Sometimes we know what we shouldn't do, or shouldn't feel, but it's hard sometimes. We're all human, and we all have failings. I mean, who has one hundred percent faith and trust at all times?"

"I wish other people knew what you know, Florence. I'm glad I came here to talk. You've made me feel so much better."

The loud sounds in the kitchen continued, and Florence tried her best to ignore them while wondering what Cherish could possibly be doing in there. "That's good, I'm glad. And how is Stephen doing?"

"He's really upset and trying not to show it. He's trying to be strong for me."

"And are you still as much in love with him as you were

the day you married him?" Florence had no idea why she asked that at a time like this.

"I'm even more in love with him now. I couldn't ever be without him."

Florence nodded. "I know what you mean."

"Are things like that with you and Carter?"

"Most definitely. But you seemed to know you were going to be in love with Stephen before you even met him."

For the first time that day, Mercy smiled. "It was a feeling, just a feeling. And I was right." Then the smile faded. "But I didn't know I was going to lose the *boppli*. Not in one million years did I consider it would happen. I didn't even think about it."

When Cherish carried the tea items in on a tray, Florence was relieved. "You found everything alright, then?"

"I did. It wasn't too difficult. I was going to make coffee but then that coffee machine looks a bit complicated."

It was then Florence realized all those loud noises were Cherish trying to operate the built-in coffee machine. Carter loved his coffee and Florence hoped Cherish hadn't broken his machine. "It's not really difficult. I can make a coffee if that's what you would prefer." She looked at each of the girls.

"Not for me." Mercy shook her head.

"Me either. Hot tea will be alright just for today."

Florence eyed her carefully. Did Cherish know the

machine was broken and was that why she said she didn't want coffee? After all, it'd be better for Cherish if someone found out the coffee machine wasn't working after she left rather than before.

"Cherish is still getting herself into trouble." Mercy giggled.

Florence nodded as she reached for her teacup. "I know. I heard about her meeting with the bishop." She looked up at Cherish. "Did you have another meeting already?"

"Jah, I did. It was with just the bishop and his wife, this time. I just said I liked Tom, but I didn't set out to do badly. Then I told him that I was out for a walk and Tom was riding by and asked if I wanted a ride."

"Wait a minute." Florence said. "Was this that same time you were both seen together at two o'clock in the morning?"

"It was."

"And, they believed what you said?"

"They did. I said it, so they believed it."

"Cherish, please be careful. Lying never got anyone anywhere. Remember that."

Cherish shrugged her shoulders. "Everyone lies to some degree."

Florence narrowed her eyes. "That's not so."

"Well, everyone's deceptive in some way at some time."

"I don't like to think that's true," Mercy said.

"Florence is deceitful. *Mamm* said so."

Florence moved uncomfortably in her seat. "What do you mean?"

"*Mamm* said you were always going to leave the community and marry an outsider and that's why you never got baptized."

"Cherish!" Mercy said. "That's totally untrue."

"It's okay. It doesn't bother me," Florence told Mercy. "I know that's not true. I'm not sure why I never got baptized. It's something I always thought I would do right before I got married. I was always committed to *Gott* in my heart, and still am. Anyway, nothing would change how some people feel about me. I know certain people aren't happy with me, but I've got a new life now. I can't let their negative thoughts or words affect me."

"Never leave us out of your new life," Mercy said. "You're our big *schweschder* and always will be."

Florence smiled, and felt better. "Before you leave, I'll give you my cell phone number for emergencies. Or, just to call if you ever want to talk."

"I'd like that, *denke.*"

"Does *Mamm* know you're here today?"

CHAPTER THIRTEEN

"*N*ee," Cherish answered. "She thinks we're walking around the orchard."

"I suspected as much."

"We didn't really mean to lie," Mercy said. "We just didn't want to upset her too much."

"That's all," added Cherish. "I told you everyone lies. It was so we wouldn't hurt her feelings, but it was still a lie."

Mercy took a sip of tea and lowered the cup to the saucer. "Anyway, I'm a grown woman. I don't have to make excuses to my *mudder*."

"But you still do," Cherish told Mercy with a giggle.

"I suppose I do. She'd say that while I'm staying under her roof I have to follow her rules. Maybe I could stay here." Mercy swiveled her head as she looked around the place.

Carter would hate it. Besides that, no one in the community would find it appropriate if Mercy stayed with her. "Maybe your bishop wouldn't like you staying with someone not in the community."

"Jah, I didn't think of that."

"Besides, this place is pretty small. We've only got one bedroom and the office." The office had been two small bedrooms—Carter had knocked out the adjoining wall and had them made into one bigger room for his office.

"You have a comfy couch," said Cherish as she bounced up and down. "I'll have to remember that if *Mamm* kicks me out."

"Don't get me involved, please," Florence said. "Better still, don't go doing silly things that will make *Mamm* cross with you."

"I'll try not to, but sometimes it's hard. Sometimes people get annoyed with me for nothing at all."

Mercy and Florence exchanged smiles. They both knew how much trouble Cherish could get herself into without even trying.

"Mamm wasn't too happy when Tom called around to see you yesterday."

"Exactly, and that wasn't my fault. I can't control what he does. I didn't even ask him or want him to come and see me."

Florence couldn't help herself. She had to offer advice. "Have you told him you're not interested in him?"

"I couldn't be so cruel as to do that."

"Maybe it would be kind. Once he knows you're not interested he can go back to Isabel and make amends."

"She wouldn't have him back, and anyway I saw her riding in Samuel Yoder's buggy the other day. It looks like she's got somebody new and that didn't take very long at all."

It was the same old dramas and Florence was glad she'd gotten away.

"Do you like it here?" asked Mercy looking around once more.

"I do like it, but it's a little sad living next door to my childhood home where I'm not welcome, and next to my orchard—and it'll always be my orchard no matter what anybody says."

"Pretty soon it'll be Levi's orchard." Cherish turned up her nose. "We'll have to take orders from him and does he even know what he's doing?"

Florence wanted to block her ears. She'd never get used to that idea. "I know and I never thought that that would happen at all." She looked over at Mercy and hoped she was feeling a little better, at least for now. "How long are you here for?"

"I'm not sure. Stephen said to stay as long as I want. I'm thinking to go back soon now I've had my visit and I'm glad I saw that you're happy. I was worried after what I'd heard about Carter. Who could believe that *Mamm* could keep a secret like that? She had a son and we have a *bruder*. I wish he would've been here for me to meet."

"I know, and I'm sorry he wasn't. You'll meet him. He's just getting used to the idea that Wilma knows who he is and … and everything." She wanted to say he was getting used to the idea of Wilma's cold-heartedness. In a funny way, he was being a little that way to his half-sisters. Couldn't he see that?

"And Carter doesn't even look like us," Cherish added. "He's so tall."

Mercy pouted. "I've never even met him and Honor has."

"Stop by tomorrow. He should be home all day. I don't think he's got any meetings."

"I would love that."

"Good, so would he."

Mercy smiled again. "It's funny that we are doubly related now through marriage as well as Dat. You're our half-sister and you've married our half-brother."

"That's right. It is a little odd."

Cherish slurped the remainder of her tea and set the cup back down onto the saucer with a loud clanging sound. "We'd better go now, Mercy, or *Mamm* will think we've been gone on an awfully long walk."

"Okay." Mercy stood up. "What time should I come back tomorrow, Florence?"

"Why don't you make it mid-morning?"

"Gut. And if *Mamm's* got something else organized for us,

I shall just tell her I'm not feeling up to it and then I'll
come and see you and Carter."

Cherish giggled loudly. "See? Everyone lies, just like I said.
I'm always right about everything."

Mercy frowned at her, and then said to Florence, "I do
hope he likes me."

"He will. Why wouldn't he? You're family after all."
Florence knew that Mercy and Stephen's baby would've
been old enough that they would've had a funeral, but
since Mercy hadn't mentioned it she wasn't going to
either.

"What are you two going to do with the rest of the day?"
Florence asked as she walked the girls to the door.

"Not much of anything, I hope," said Mercy. "I just want
to have a rest."

"Ada and Samuel are coming for dinner and also Isaac, as
usual. Joy's cooking."

"As usual," Mercy repeated, which made Cherish giggle.

"Not much has changed then," Florence said.

"That's right, except Levi and Bliss will be there as well.
They're at the *haus* nearly every other day for dinner."

"You better get used to it because soon they'll be there
every day for dinner."

Cherish made a grumbling sound from the back of her
throat. "I can't wait to get out on my own. Bliss was nice

once but now she's treating me like I'm an idiot just because I'm younger than she is. And, she better not be thinking it means she can boss me around after the wedding."

"Don't worry about it. Everyone will have some adjusting to do."

"I'm not worried. As soon as I'm old enough I'm going to go back to my farm."

Spot jumped off the couch, walked over to them and sat by Florence's feet.

The girls told him goodbye and he just stared up at them. He didn't seem too trusting of strangers. When Cherish put a hand out to pat him, he lowered his head and looked up at her showing the whites of his eyes.

Cherish removed her hand. "He won't bite, will he?"

"No. At least I don't think so. He's generally pretty mild-mannered."

"I think he's an old dog. That's why he doesn't have much energy. Not like Goldie and Caramel."

Florence patted him. "He's a funny dog."

"Yes, he is. I thought he was going to bite me there for a second."

"I'll give you my number." Florence found pen and paper and quickly scribbled her number down twice and gave a note to each girl.

When they had said their goodbyes, Florence crouched down beside Spot and they both watched the girls leave.

"It's just you and me now, Spot, at least until daddy gets home." Spot turned to her and without warning, gave her a huge lick up the side of the face. She moved away. "Agh. Don't do that."

The coffee machine!

CHAPTER FOURTEEN

*O*nce Florence saw her sisters had gotten safely back through the fence, she hurried to the kitchen to see if Cherish had broken anything. There were sections of the coffee machine strewn across the countertop, along with damp lumps of coffee grinds. Florence picked up each piece of the contraption and looked to see if any of it was dented.

Everything looked fine.

She heaved a sigh of relief.

She would've hated to tell Carter his coffee machine had been ruined. She pulled out the instructions and put all the sections back together carefully, and then cleaned up the mess that Cherish had left. It reminded her of how things used to be, with her constantly cleaning up after the girls, day in and day out.

She walked to the other room and got their tray of tea

items, brought them back into the kitchen and placed the cups and saucers into the dishwasher.

A dishwasher was the best thing ever invented. Florence giggled to herself. All the dirty dishes went into the dishwasher and then the place would be clean within moments. A quick wipe down of the counters and the sink and the place looked pristine—as good as new. And, when the machine was full, add a little detergent, push a couple buttons, wait a short time and—like magic—clean dishes! She giggled again as she walked back out to the living room and sat next to Spot.

"We've got a free day to ourselves Spot. I wonder what we should do."

There was so much to do in preparing the soil for the orchard that Florence barely knew where to start. Making a list of what to do was as far as she'd gotten.

She also felt somewhat unmotivated since being shunned from her own orchard. Carter had mentioned moving away and she wondered if that might not be the better thing to do. However, was moving away practical, now that he had bought up much of the surrounding land to create an orchard? Also, he'd bought the Jenkins' orchard, which gave them a small head start on production.

She stroked Spot's white and black fur.

"We'll simply have to stay here, Spot, and we'll make the best of it. We'll create a brand-new orchard, bigger and better than anything around here. The only thing is, we'll need workers. Perhaps I could pay *Dat's* old friend to oversee the project? He's done that for others." She'd suggest that to Carter.

Florence spotted Carter's laptop on the other side of the room. She fetched it and sat down with it on her lap. The night before, he'd been showing her how to play chess on the app he and his team had created. It seemed a complicated game and rather a waste of time. She closed the lid and put it back where she found it.

Then she went up to their bedroom to get her needlework to fill in time while Carter was out. Unlike chess, when she finished her needlework she had something to show for it. When you finished a game of chess, you had nothing. She'd rather play a game with another person, like the card games they used to play as a family before their Bible readings. That was what they'd done when *Dat* was still alive. Her life and so many things in the family had changed after his death.

When she found her sampler in one of her drawers, she noticed the letter her mother had written to her.

She sat down on the bed with the letter in her hands and then she held it close to her chest. Her mother had touched the same page. It was the only significant reminder she had of the mother she could barely remember.

It renewed within her a desire to learn more about her. Now that she had left the Amish, she couldn't ask anybody in the community about her mother, so she had to find someone outside of the community—some relatives, or some friends.

She spent the next two hours sewing, waiting for Carter to come home.

CARTER OPENED the front door and called out, "Is the coast clear?"

She dropped the sewing into her lap at the same time as Spot jumped off the couch and ran to meet him.

"They've come and gone."

"Thank heavens for that."

She giggled. He patted Spot, walked over and kissed her on the forehead and then sat down next to her.

"And what have you been doing today, Mrs. Braithwaite?"

"A bit of this, a bit of that. I've been doing some more thinking about my mother."

"I've got somebody on the trail already. It's a little difficult, though, since I don't have much to go on."

"I know. Joy said she'd see that Isaac brought the boxes in the attic to me. That hasn't happened yet."

"These people helped me find my mother, so they'll be able to help me find yours."

"Thank you."

"How was Mercy?"

"Distraught. Thoroughly distraught, as she would be."

"It's very sad."

She was pleased he was softening, somewhat. "She's coming back tomorrow to see you. She's never met you."

He sat straighter and smiled. "She wants to meet me?"

"Yes, she does. She seemed to like the idea of having another brother."

"Good. Then, I'd like to meet her."

Florence giggled. "You'll like her."

"She's the oldest?"

"That's right."

"I'm looking forward to it."

CHAPTER FIFTEEN

The next day, Mercy came to visit Carter. After a while, Florence left them alone to talk. While she was by herself, her thoughts turned to Earl. She'd heard nothing from him.

Had he received her letter?

Or, perhaps he wanted nothing to do with her since she had left the community.

When Mercy left, and Carter went into his study to do some work, Florence walked outside and called Earl from her cell phone. He worked in a lumberyard, and she was so pleased when he was the one to answer the phone.

"Earl, it's me, Florence."

There was silence on the other end of the line and Florence held her breath hoping he wouldn't end the call.

"Florence, I wasn't expecting to hear from you after your letter."

"So, you did get the letter?"

"Yes, I'm sorry I haven't replied yet. Things have been pretty hectic around here. I've made a couple of attempts."

"You're still talking to me, then?"

He chuckled. "Of course I am. You'll always be my sister and I'll always talk to you. I know we haven't kept in touch as much as we should over the years, but you're in my thoughts every day."

She got teary eyed when he said that. "And you're in mine. Even though we're apart."

"Who is this man you married?"

She giggled. "Have you got time to talk?"

"All the time in the world. I'm in on my break right now."

"It sounds like you haven't heard the full story."

"I've heard bits and pieces. Tell me everything."

"Wilma obviously doesn't want this to get out, but since you're part of the family you should probably know."

"What's happened?"

"Nothing, but something happened many years ago."

"Tell me."

"Wilma had a baby before she dated and married *Dat.* She had a baby in secret and then adopted him out."

"Is that right?"

"It is." She started walking slowly instead of standing still.

She was too used to the phone in the barn that was attached by a cord. *This is better,* she thought, liking to be able to walk around while talking.

"I find that hard, very hard to believe."

"It's true." She had hoped he'd heard more so she wouldn't have to be the one to tell him.

"When did you find out?"

"Only very recently because, Carter, the man I married, is the child she adopted out."

"No!"

"That's right."

"That's hard to believe."

"I can barely believe it myself but it's true." She glanced back at the house.

"You've married our stepmother's illegitimate child?"

"Well, it's not something I set out to do, believe me."

"How did Wilma find him?"

"It's not like that at all. She didn't want to find him. In fact, she won't even speak to him. Well, barely."

He grunted. "I'm not surprised. Nothing she does amazes me."

She wasn't sure what he meant, but neither did she want to ask. She'd save that topic for another time.

"I hope you thought this decision through, Florence."

"Leaving the community, or marrying?"

"Jah, and *jah*—both of those things."

"I thought it through. It's not something I would ever do lightly. You know me."

"I do. That's why I was surprised to get your letter. You were so entrenched with the family orchard. I thought nothing or nobody would ever get you away from it. I thought you'd marry and live at the orchard, have your husband move there too and live in the *haus* with Wilma."

She gave a little giggle. "I probably would've, but nothing turned out that way. I'll give you my cell phone number."

"I have it. You put it in your letter."

"Oh, good. I'm glad you're still talking to me."

"Always."

"While I've got you on the phone, do you remember anything about our mother?"

He replied quickly, "Not much, no, not much at all."

Closing her eyes, she hoped he knew something. "Did you know that she wasn't raised in the Amish community?"

"That explains a lot."

"Explains what?"

"That explains why we never had any relatives on her side."

"I never really thought about it too much. Nobody ever spoke about her and I thought that was a little weird.

Then I thought no one wanted to speak about her in front of Wilma, with her being the second wife and all. Anyway, I'm going to find out more. Find a relative of hers."

"Let me know as soon as you find out anything."

"I will, but do you even know her last name—her maiden name?"

"I can't say that I ever heard it. And now that you talk about it, I can't think why I didn't ask more questions. Anyway, my break's over. Your call was good timing."

"I'm glad. Bye, Earl."

"I'll hear from you soon, *jah?*"

"Yes. And you can call me, too." She ended the call, went back into the house and sat down by Spot. She placed the phone beside her and leaned back on the couch. It was such a relief to know that Earl was still talking to her. Neither of her brothers had turned his back on her and it felt good.

Now for those boxes. She had to get those boxes from the attic to get her mother's papers. Joy had either forgotten or Wilma had forbidden those items of her mother's to leave the house.

Maybe something had happened?

Something bad.

No. Mercy would've mentioned it.

"Carter, I'm going for a walk," she called out, loud enough for him to hear.

SAMANTHA PRICE

"Okay. I'll be done with this in a couple of hours. Then we can talk to Eric Brosley about overseeing preparing the orchard."

She'd mentioned that idea last night and he agreed it sounded good. "Okay. I hope he agrees."

"Me too."

Carter's money was certainly coming in handy. It would take a long time before they made a profit. That was why buying the Jenkins' orchard had been a good idea.

She closed the door behind her so Spot would stay inside. The last thing she wanted was to hear Wilma complaining about another dog on her property.

She slipped through the fence and made her way through her old orchard.

Her intention was to see what was going on at the house, see who was visiting, or get a sense of what was going on.

When she got closer to the house, she saw there were no visiting buggies.

That meant Levi wasn't there.

Good.

Then she spotted Cherish behind the house pinning up the washing. The house seemed so still and quiet. Maybe all the girls had gone out with Wilma, all but Cherish. There was nobody else, except for the two dogs chasing one another in circles.

She crouched down and watched Cherish for a while. It

114

was odd to see Cherish doing chores. She normally found a way to get out of them.

It seemed odd for someone so lazy to be suddenly blessed with being left Aunt Dagmar's farm.

Shouldn't the hard-working people be rewarded instead?

God had a plan, that was obvious. A plan for Cherish's life, and it had something to do with the farm.

She stood up to go back to her house and right at that moment, Cherish spotted her. Florence waved, hoping that Cherish wouldn't yell out.

Instead, the dress in Cherish's hands dropped to the ground and then she ran toward her. Florence was nearly knocked off her feet when Cherish flung her arms around her.

"What are you doing here, Florence? Have you come to make amends with *Mamm?*"

"I don't think that's possible. We'll never see things the same."

"Then, why are you here?"

"I was just worried, that's all. I asked Joy to bring me some things from the house and she said she would have Isaac bring them, but I've heard nothing."

"What things?"

"I've got my mother's boxes in the attic."

"I could bring them to you."

"Could you?"

Cherish nodded enthusiastically.

"There's such a lot, but the main thing I want is the paper-work. Wedding certificate, birth certificate, anything like that with her name on it. If you just bring me those things, I can get everything else at a later time."

"Those are the urgent things you're after, *jah?*"

"That's right."

Cherish put her arms behind her back. "You must want them pretty bad."

"I do. It's quite urgent."

"So ... if I do that for you, would you do something for me?"

CHAPTER SIXTEEN

*F*lorence studied Cherish's face. *She hasn't changed a bit.* She'd always been scheming and calculating. "What do you want me to do for you?"

Cherish shook her head after she'd looked Florence up and down. "I can't get used to seeing you in those clothes. Anyway, I need to go back to the farm. It's being ruined by that stupid caretaker."

"He seemed very competent. Why would you think differently?"

"I heard some things. I've got people looking out for me and they told me what he's been doing."

"And what has he been doing that you're so worried about?"

Cherish pouted. "He's sold some of the cows and bought more goats."

"He'd only be doing that because he'd be able to work

things better that way. When we were there he did talk about that to you."

"Exactly, and I told him I wanted things to stay exactly the same as Aunt Dagmar had them."

"Do you want me to drive you there?"

Cherish nodded. "Please."

"I can't drive. I'd have to get Carter to drive us."

"Can't you do that?"

Florence amazed herself by not finding the idea too bad. "We'd have to stay at a B&B somewhere. We couldn't inconvenience him."

Cherish's face lit up. "Or just drive up for the day and come back."

"I'll think about it." Florence wasn't certain if she could talk Carter into it.

The smile left Cherish's lips. "And I'll *think about* getting you those papers."

"Are you really blackmailing me right now, Cherish Baker?"

"I believe it's called bribery, and yes. Isn't it blackmailing when someone gets money out of someone? Like if I would say I won't tell *Mamm* I gave you those papers if you give me one hundred dollars?"

Florence rolled her eyes. "Like I said, I'll have to think about it. I'll get those things I talked about some other way. Thanks, Cherish."

She turned and walked away. Cherish called after her, "I'm really worried, Florence, and you're the only one who can help me. We can help each other."

"Like I said, I'll think about it. I'll need to talk to Carter and see if he can take a couple of days off work."

"Thanks, Florence, you're the best."

"We'll talk about it later."

"I'll come to your house tomorrow."

"Okay." Florence walked away not sure whether she would ever get her mother's papers.

Cherish would probably bring them with her tomorrow, and hold them over her head until she agreed with her demands.

THE NEXT DAY, there was no sign of Cherish and Florence was upset. She turned to Carter for comfort. She told him about their conversation the day before.

"It's kind of irritating being so close to where I moved away from. Would we lose money if we just picked up and left? You mentioned it before."

"I'd like to say we wouldn't, but we would. I paid more than what the properties were worth because I thought this area meant something to you."

Florence felt awful. "And I appreciate that and it does, it's just that it also holds memories and I just wondered if we're better off away from here."

"Do you think distance is the answer? You're here with me. This is as good a place as any to start our life together. This was your father's land and this cottage is now yours."

"That's true."

"Don't let them ruin this for you—for us."

What he said made perfect sense. "I do like it here. The truth is I'm just a bit daunted by all the work ahead of me."

"I know what you're thinking. It would've been much easier just to go ahead with running your orchard next door."

"That's right. You said I never opened up to you, so now I'm doing that."

"That's good. We've got to communicate with each other so we know what the other is thinking. Never shut me out or hide things just to keep me happy."

She nodded. "I think I tend to do that. That's what I did with the girls all the time."

"You're not with the girls, you don't have to look after me. I'm the one looking after you, remember?"

She looked into his serious eyes and saw all the love he had for her. "I know. I'm getting used to that and it's a nice feeling."

"Good."

"Yes, very good." She stepped into him and he wrapped his arms around her.

"We're moving forward, not backward. The orchard next door is in your past and this land is our future and the future of our children whenever they decide to appear."

She giggled. "I hope that's soon."

"I'm in no rush. There's more time to spend with you."

THE NEXT FEW months flew by with Florence having no word from her family.

In those months, Florence and Carter's land hadn't changed. They'd learned that it would take several months of ground preparation before they could proceed. The soil had been tested, and now extensive drainage systems had to be constructed. Carter had already given his cows away to someone close by who agreed never to kill them and they allowed Carter to visit them whenever he wanted.

Finally, Cherish knocked on their door one morning.

"Ah," Florence said as she looked her in the eye. "I hope you haven't forgotten my mother's papers?"

"Oh, I'm sorry. I forgot. Is it important?"

"Yes. You said you'd come here the next day after we talked. I was all set to take you up there to the farm."

"Sorry, I've been busy. Levi told *Mamm* I should get a job.

Instead of us opening a stall, she sent me out to find a real job."

Florence leaned against the doorpost not sure if she wanted Cherish to come inside. "Where are you working?"

"At a boring café. Customers are so demanding. They don't understand how hard it is to remember everything and to give them the correct change, and everything. It's difficult."

"It shouldn't be more difficult than when we had the stall at the farmers market."

"Much, much harder than that. That was easy."

"Oh."

"Won't you please take me to the farm? I beg you."

"What about your job?"

"I can take some time off. I work different shifts. Not every day."

"And, what about *Mamm?* What will she say if Carter and I drive you to the farm?"

Cherish screwed up her nose. *"Mamm* doesn't care if you take me. I asked her and she said she doesn't care what I do anymore. She says she's given up on me." After a huge sigh, Cherish continued, "Now she's blaming me for Tom splitting up with Isabel, but it wasn't my fault. I wasn't even here when he did it. They ended their relationship on the same day as Aunt Dagmar's funeral."

"I'll ask Carter, but I do need my mother's papers."

Cherish nodded. "No one's been up in the attic. They're still there. I'll get them for you. I will whether you take me or not."

"Thank you. Well, I'll talk to Carter when he gets home and then I'll have to see if it's okay with Wilma."

"I said it will be."

"I'll need to ask her myself."

"Okay. *Denke,* Florence. She leaned forward and hugged her. Florence patted her back. "I'll be late for work if I don't go. I'll check back with you tomorrow."

"Bye."

CHAPTER SEVENTEEN

"*Y*ou promised what?" Carter ran a hand over his short hair.

Were her sisters coming between her and the man she loved? "Are you upset?"

"I'm not upset. I'm surprised. I'm trying to keep you away from all the dramas, to give you a better life. That was the deal when we got married, remember?"

"I know and I don't want to be drawn into anything either, but they are my family … and they're your family, don't forget that."

"I'm not forgetting that. Okay, what's the plan?"

"We go there and have a look at the place and set Cherish's mind at rest. She's really young, remember, not even sixteen yet, and she must feel incredible responsibility to keep Aunt Dagmar's farm and *haus* nice."

"You've got a point. And what about Wilma? How would

she feel about us driving her youngest daughter somewhere?"

"According to Cherish, she doesn't care about her any more. It seems Wilma's lost total control and she told her she could do whatever she liked. But she didn't say it so politely."

"I see, according to Cherish, eh?"

Florence smiled. "I know she's bent the truth before, but this time I almost believe her."

"Once we hear, directly from Wilma, that she doesn't mind us driving her, I'm okay with it."

"Really?"

"Whatever makes you happy."

"Really?"

He stepped closer and held her tight. "Yes, dear wife, really. Really!"

"I'll find out from Wilma if it's okay. I'll walk over and see her now."

"Good. And when is this planned for?"

"The day after tomorrow."

FLORENCE WALKED up to her old house. She couldn't see anyone about and she secretly hoped they were all out. When she arrived at the front door, she paused. It seemed odd that she would have to knock on the door of her family home especially when many of her family members were still living inside. If *Dat* had never married again, this place would be hers and her brothers. Now, it might as well belong to a stranger. Life could be so unfair sometimes.

Before she could knock, Wilma opened it and there was an awkward moment with the two women staring at one another.

"Hello, Wilma."

Instead of answering, Wilma gave a curt nod.

It was no surprise she wasn't invited inside. "Cherish asked me if Carter and I can drive her back to the farm. She's worried about it."

Wilma shrugged her shoulders. "She hasn't stopped talking about anything else. If you want to drive her, it will save us money on a car and driver to take her."

"You don't mind?" Florence had been certain she'd say no.

"A few days without Cherish here will do everyone a world of good. She's already told us she doesn't like us and as soon as she's old enough she's leaving to go and live on *her* farm. That farm should never have been left to Cherish. Aunt Dagmar made a terrible mistake; one that we're all paying for."

"We'll leave the day after tomorrow, very early. Cherish will have to be at our place at five in the morning."

"I'll let her know."

"Thank you." Florence pushed some strands of hair away

from her face and then Wilma fixed her eyes onto her gold wedding band.

Wilma didn't have to say a word; the expression on her face said it all. Not only had she cut her hair, she was wearing jewelry.

"How is Levi doing with the orchard?"

"I don't wish to discuss it with you, Florence. We really have nothing more to say to one another."

Once, Florence had desperately wanted to be loved by Wilma as much as her stepmother loved her "own" daughters. It had never happened.

"Well, that's all I came to ask."

"You've asked and I've given my permission. Goodbye, Florence."

"Goodbye." Florence turned and walked away. She hadn't even gotten to the bottom step of the porch when she heard the front door close. She glanced over her shoulder at the door.

Wilma had shut her out.

Florence tried to quell her feelings of bitterness.

It wasn't easy.

Cherish had been right. The only reason Wilma was allowing Cherish to go with her and Carter was she didn't care about her at all. In fact, all she wanted was for Cherish to be gone. She couldn't blame Wilma for that. Cherish could be a real handful. She walked away from the house realizing she'd missed an opportunity to ask about her mother's paperwork.

It made sense to go back and ask, but Florence's legs kept moving away.

As she walked through the orchard, she wanted to cry for all of the times Wilma had slighted her and used her and hurt her, but the tears wouldn't come.

WHEN FLORENCE and Carter were about halfway to Aunt Dagmar's farm with Cherish riding in the backseat, Carter said to Cherish, "Can I make a suggestion?"

Cherish leaned forward as far as her seat belt would allow. "Yes?" She had been complaining about Malachi the whole trip and Florence knew that Carter couldn't take it anymore.

"This is the man that you chose to look after your property. Can you reserve your judgement until you get there and see what's going on?"

"Oh, is that your suggestion?"

"Yes."

"I thought you were going to suggest a way to get rid of him."

Florence stifled a giggle. "I think what Carter is saying is not to cross your bridges before you come to them."

"I know in my heart he's run the farm down and that's

why I'm so upset. If I've been talking too much, I'm sorry, but I'm just worried and I thought we were all family here."

"We are and we'll help you if we need to do anything but there's no good in complaining about things until you know the facts."

"Florence is right. That's what I'm trying to tell you, Cherish," Carter said.

"I'm not a child, I own a farm and should be treated with respect."

"I'm just trying to tell you, as your older half-brother, not to worry so much. You're working yourself up and things might not be that bad."

Cherish blew out a deep breath and pushed back in the seat. "Okay I'll keep quiet then."

"Is that even possible?" Carter asked.

"Just as long as you help me get rid of him if I want to, and find somebody else. Will you?"

"Who are you talking to, me, or Carter?"

"I was talking to Carter mainly, sorry Florence, but you were the one who thought it was a good idea to choose him."

"Yes, but we had no reason to think that it wasn't a good idea, and we really didn't have a lot of choice if you'll remember."

"I've got a pretty good idea that it was a bad idea."

"See? I told you that you wouldn't keep quiet."

"And what if he's had other people staying there that I don't know about?"

"There you go again worrying about unknown things."

"Yeah, but … I don't know. I just want both of you on my side in case I have to get rid of him. The worst thing would be that if I want to get rid of him and you both think he's suitable. Then you'll tell me that I'm too young to know what I'm talking about and yet it's my farm." Cherish leaned forward. "So, what do you think about that?"

Carter said nothing. He slowed the car, and then stopped at the side of the road.

"What are you doing?" Florence asked.

"Stopping the car."

"I can see that, but why?"

"I'm only going to drive when Cherish stops talking. As soon as you talk, Cherish, I'm going to stop again."

"That's not fair! How far is it now?"

"We're about halfway," Florence said.

"You want me to not talk the rest of the way?"

"That's right. Each time you talk I'm going to stop."

"What do you think, Florence. Are you going to allow him to do that to me?"

"He is the driver, and neither of us can drive."

"I'll be quiet."

"Only talk if it's an emergency," Florence said.

"I can see what's going on here. You're both against me."

"You're not acting like an adult, Cherish. All this constant chatter is getting on my nerves. You worry about nothing. You're seriously worried about nothing and it's doing my head in."

"Okay I'll be quiet on the way, as long as you help me get rid of him when we get there."

"Let's just see what's happened before we make any plans, shall we?"

"Okay. Drive on and I'll do my best to keep quiet."

THE REST of the way there, they'd only had to stop two more times. Both times Cherish had forgotten she wasn't supposed to talk.

When they finally arrived, Cherish hurried out of the car ahead of Florence and Carter. She was determined to find out what was going on and to be the first one to do so.

Malachi walked out of the house and leaned on the porch railing.

He looked the same. The same tall and skinny man with the eyes as black as a winter's night.

Cherish certainly didn't know why Florence had said he was handsome.

"Ah, you brought people with ya."

"Hello to you too."

He straightened up. "Hiya, Cherish."

"Well, at least you got my name right this time. I brought my sister with me again, and her husband."

He grinned at her. "You didn't bring Timmy back for a visit?"

"No."

"How's he getting along?"

Cherish was annoyed the way he was smirking at her and asking about Timmy as though they were friends. He'd only seen Timmy for five minutes. "Why would you care about Timmy, a bird you've hardly seen?"

He scratched his chin. "I was just being polite."

He had a day's growth of beard and his clothes, as usual, hadn't been pressed. He looked a mess. "I didn't bring Timmy and I didn't bring my dog, Caramel, either. Because my ... Carter has a very nice car. It looks quite expensive, and I didn't think you would want me bringing Caramel with me."

"That's very thoughtful of you."

"And are you surprised about that?" Cherish folded her arms across her chest.

"Not surprised at all. You seem a very thoughtful, kind and caring woman."

"Woman? That's right, I'm a woman and don't you forget it."

He sniggered. "I wasn't about to."

She stepped up to the porch and looked up at him. "Now tell me about the farm. What have you done? I've heard some disturbing things from Ruth next door."

"Oh, her. She doesn't like me very much." He leaned in toward her and whispered, "She hates me, I'd reckon."

"What a surprise."

"I know. Shocking really."

"She tells me you've been selling off livestock and buying different ones."

"She ain't lyin.'"

Cherish huffed. "When I left, I sent specific instructions for you to keep everything as it was, do you remember that?"

He scratched the back of his head tipping his hat forwards slightly on his head. Then he straightened up and pushed his hat back. "Can't recall. Sorry."

"You must recall it. I was very clear in my instructions to you. You talked about wanting to do what you've done and I said no, I didn't want that."

"But now that I've done it, you'll see that everything works out better." He smiled a wide grin. She couldn't help noticing how straight and perfect his teeth were. It nearly made up for the rest of him.

"I want to be the one to change things when I move here and see what needs doing."

"You can always change what I've done if you think it's not good."

She sighed. "You'd better show me the damage you've done."

"Okay, but first let me say hello to Florence and Carter." He left her without saying another word and headed directly to Florence and Carter.

Cherish waited there at the front of the house trying to quell her anger. She couldn't remember the last time she'd been so annoyed. When he finished talking to Florence and Carter, he walked back. "They insist on staying at a bed-and-breakfast. Will you talk to them and tell them they should stay here?"

"Clearly, I have no influence over people. You don't listen to me, so what makes you think they'll listen to me?"

"Ah, smart. Smart as well as pretty." He grinned at her and she rolled her eyes.

"Just show me the damage done, will you?"

"I can't show you damage, but I can show ya the positive changes I've made."

"Same thing."

"Come along." He strode ahead and she hurried to catch up with him.

. . .

FLORENCE LOOKED over at Carter "Do you think we should stay here? It's a big house."

"It's up to you. I thought you would be more comfortable staying at a bed-and-breakfast."

"It doesn't matter to me. When Cherish finishes talking, I'll see what she wants to do. I'm sure she'd want to stay here so she can keep a closer eye on what's happening. So maybe we should stay, too, as chaperones or whatever."

"Sure, I'm happy to do whatever you want."

"I'm sure he wouldn't mind if we go in and make ourselves a cup of coffee or something."

"Let's do it. And I wouldn't mind a ten-minute snooze on the couch after all that driving."

CHERISH SNIFFED the air as they walked past the barn. "What's that revolting smell?

"There's a smell yes, but it's not revolting. It's strong, and there's no way to avoid that. I'm making and selling goat's cheese. There's a huge demand and it brings a very good price. That's why I sold some of the cows and bought more goats."

"I thought you'd like cows. Didn't you tell me one of your *onkels* owned a dairy and you worked on it?"

He beamed at her. "You remembered."

She looked away from him. "I thought you'd get more cows if anything."

"Gotta do what brings in the money. You'll thank me for it one day."

Shaking her head, she said, "I don't think so. It's awful—the smell. I wish you would've asked me first."

"Why is it that we never agree on anything, Cherish?"

"That's because we're very different people, you and I."

He nodded and held on to one side of his suspenders. "I'm thankful for that."

"Hey, that's not nice."

He grinned, and then leaned down and plucked a grass stem and popped one end of it in his mouth. "You know I'm not serious."

"How would I know that?" She liked the way he wasn't offended by anything she said. She could say anything and he'd still smile at her. "I say things I don't mean sometimes. I don't mean to be cruel, it's just that I'm impatient sometimes."

"And perhaps a little ... oh, spoiled?"

She put her hands on her hips. "Who told you that?"

"Nobody told me nothing,' didn't need to." He twirled the grass around while keeping the end in his mouth.

"Someone had to have told you that I'm spoiled."

He threw his head back and laughed. "I'm not sure what you mean, but I'm just going on what I see meself."

"I probably used to be spoiled, but that's not my fault

anyway now my mother says she doesn't care about me. She said I'm selfish and she doesn't care what happens to me. And she didn't even care that I was coming back to the farm with Florence. Florence left the community to marry Carter. He's so nice and they're so well-suited."

"I figured that much out for meself, her dressed in her *Englisch* clothes and the short hair. I hope she's happy."

"You're a very strange man, Malachi."

"Thank you."

"It wasn't a compliment."

"I didn't think it was."

He threw the grass stem to the ground and stared at her, and they both laughed. Then just as quickly she stopped. She didn't want to get along too well with him because then he would think he could do anything he liked on the farm. No, she had to keep a decent distance from him.

"So, are you happy with what I've done?"

"No. I told you that already. I mean, it's not too awful. Not as bad as I was expecting." She looked at the empty chicken coop. "Wait a minute, where are my chickens?"

"About that. You see, I didn't think it was a very good idea to keep chickens."

"Why not? Don't you eat eggs?"

He licked his lips. "I do, that's not the problem."

"Why would you sell my chickens? That makes no sense. Wait, did you eat them?"

"No, I didn't. I gave them away."

"You what?" Cherish screeched.

"In exchange for a goat."

"So, you gave up a food source for a smelly goat?"

He blew out a deep breath.

"Now to get eggs, you have to buy them."

"I have a problem with chickens."

Cherish stared at him. "What problem could you possibly have with chickens?"

"You'll laugh."

"I can tell you right now I will not laugh. I'm very angry about you selling … or exchanging my chickens and there's nothing funny about it."

"I'm scared of nothin' except chickens."

He spoke the words so fast she could barely understand him. "What? It sounded like you said you were … scared? Of chickens?"

"That's right, always have been. When I was a small child, they used to chase me. It was terrifying. My mother laughed."

She couldn't keep the smile from her face at the vision it conjured in her mind of a small chubby-legged Malachi running away from hens. "You're scared of small chickens?"

"They weren't so tiny when I was a kid. Those chickens

were whoppers. Hugest ones I ever seen."

She held her stomach and laughed.

"See, I told you you'd laugh. It wasn't practical to keep chickens when I can't go anywhere near 'em."

"You could've just told me that when I showed you around the place."

He shook his head. "I couldn't. You wouldn't have thought much of me, then."

"Believe me, it hasn't altered my opinion of you one little bit."

He stared at her and raised his eyebrows just slightly. She looked around. "Are there any other animals that you have phobias about?"

"No, just chickens."

"Good to know."

"I'll show you the new fence I made."

They walked to one side of the farm where he showed her a brand new, post-and-wire fence. She knew exactly how much work would've gone into it and she was impressed. She had done some fence repairs with Aunt Dagmar and she knew that the fences on the property weren't very good. "I suppose you haven't done a terrible job."

"Thank you. Coming from you *that's* a compliment."

She didn't like the way he looked so smug right now. "I'm going to visit Ruth tomorrow."

The smile vanished from his face. "That old … that neighbor from next door—that Ruth?"

"Jah, that's the one. I'll tell her not to worry and I'll say that I think you're doing a reasonable job."

"Hmm, hopefully that will appease her and she'll stop spying on me."

"You think she's spying on you?"

"I don't *think* she's spying, I know she is."

"Alright, well, there's no point discussing that. I will tell her you're doing fine; it won't matter if I stretch the truth a little bit. How does that sound?"

He chuckled. "It's pretty good, coming from you."

"Very good. Let's go back to the house. I need water." She walked off and he hurried to walk beside her.

"How often do you expect that you'll be coming here for these unexpected visits?"

"I'm not certain. Otherwise they wouldn't be 'unexpected,' now would they?"

He rubbed his chin. "Will you come here every three months?"

"Jah, probably about that. Four times a year just to check up on you."

"There's really no need."

"It will put my mind at ease if I do. It was very nice of you to let us stay here. I think Florence was expecting to find a B&B somewhere."

"I'll make some beds up," he said. "Unless you want—"

"Perfect. Thank you." She took a last look at the deserted chicken coop when she walked past. "Please don't pull this down because I intend to have chickens when I move back."

"I'll leave it as I found it. Except I'll give it a good cleaning."

"Very good. Finally, something we agree on. Florence brought some food. I'll cook the dinner tonight if that's okay with you."

"Go right ahead. I'll cancel me plans."

She looked up at him. "You had plans?"

"Nah, it was a joke."

"Oh."

THAT NIGHT they had a nice meal and the conversation was kept away from the changes Malachi had made on the farm. Cherish was making a special effort to keep quiet after Carter had been upset with her for talking too much in the car.

CHAPTER EIGHTEEN

"*J*'m off to see Ruth from next door this morning."

"I'll drive you. It's a distance," Malachi said.

"I'll walk."

"Can I talk to you before you go, Cherish?"

"Sure. After breakfast."

Malachi nodded.

Cherish knew what he was worried about. He wanted to be sure that she said nice things about him.

Once the washing up was done, he walked outside with her. He brought her to a wooden bench under a large tree.

"Sit down. I'm about to teach ya a few life lessons."

She sat, but she didn't like his tone of voice. "Well since you're about the same age as I am, I don't see what lessons you could possibly have to teach me that I don't know already."

He sat beside her, shrugged, and clutched his hands together. "On a farm, if you're not moving forward, you're going backward. You have to continually change doing things. Your aunt would've done the same. Replacing animals as they died off, having one more of this, and one more of that, slightly less of this."

"What are you talking about, this and that? You're trying to sound smart, but you're really not saying anything at all."

"What I'm saying is that there's a flow to things and if ya don't go with that flow, things won't go as well."

"You're just saying that so I'll let you do anything you want, but I won't." She flew to her feet.

And then he stood up and towered over her. "Listen here, Charity, you might think you know—"

"The name's Cherish and you better get that right to start with." She wagged a finger in his face.

His frown turned into a smile. And then he laughed.

"What's so funny?" she asked.

"You are, when you pretend to get angry."

"I am angry. I'm angry for real."

"I reckon someone like you never gets angry. I reckon you're pretending, just to get your way."

"My *vadder* always used to say people judge others by

144

what they would do. Does that mean that you were pretending to be angry just now?"

He placed his hands on his hips. "What do you think?"

"I try not to think about you at all, if you really want to know."

He chuckled and tipped his hat back slightly on his head.

Then he looked over at her, "When I did what I did, I didn't do it to upset you. I did it because you put me in charge of the farm and I saw that as the right thing to do for you, for me, and for the good of the farm."

She took a step closer to him and looked up into his midnight black eyes. "I never said you could change one thing. Remember? In fact, I told you not to change *anything.*"

"I know what you said, but the trouble is that women aren't as practical as men. That's why *Gott* made men to be farmers and women to do the indoors work."

"That's just an outrageous thing to say. Just because we choose to do that doesn't mean we can't do anything else. Florence does a *wunderbaar* job of running the orchard. Just as *gut* as our *Dat.* Well, she used to, and there are many women back in my community who run successful businesses."

"You'd say anything to win an argument, wouldn't ya?"

"Just have some respect, will you? I'm only trying to preserve what my dear aunt left me." She felt tears coming to her eyes. She'd slept in Dagmar's room last night amongst all her aunt's possessions. It was weird without her there.

"Yes, and I'm saying your farm is a living thing and I'm trying to keep it going, keep it profitable for both our sakes."

"You're useless. I have to see Ruth." She hurried away so he wouldn't see the tears that were still threatening.

SHE WALKED the fifteen minutes to Ruth's farm.

Ruth, their non-Amish neighbor, came running out to meet her and hugged her. "Here you are."

"I told you I'd come back."

"I think he's doing a good job, Cherish. I know you were worried. Apart from a couple of little things that annoyed me, but apart from those things, he's doing a good job. You don't need to worry, truly you don't."

"I'm so relieved."

"Let's talk about it over a bowl of soup."

"Not for me. I've just had breakfast." They'd had pancakes for breakfast since there were no eggs, thanks to Malachi's chicken phobia. She wouldn't tell Ruth about that.

"You can talk to me while I have some."

"Okay."

. . .

As RUTH SAT at the kitchen table slurping soup, Cherish asked, "What's been happening 'round here?"

"Nothing out of the ordinary." Then she set her spoon down. "If anything happens next door, I want you to tell me first. I'll give you my phone number later."

"I already have your phone number. Why are you so interested in next door?"

"Because it's next door. I feel better knowing what's going on around here. Do you know what I mean?"

Cherish nodded, wondering why Ruth was so nosy. "I appreciate you calling me to tell me about him selling the cows. He should've been the one to tell me before he did it."

"I don't know what sort of funny goings-on are happening there with that girl he's got there all the time."

"Girl? What girl?"

"She's one of you."

"She's Amish?"

"That's right. Every time I go past I think about you there. And I know it's not Dagmar's old buggy horse because it's a darker color."

"I wonder who that could be? He must have a girlfriend, but he hasn't said anything to me about it."

"No, he wouldn't, would he? A pretty girl like you, I reckon he's probably thinking he's going to marry you when you get older. You've already got a farm and all."

Cherish was disappointed. Is that why Malachi was so nice and polite to her, even when she wasn't nice to him? He wanted to marry her one day for her farm? "We don't even like each other."

"Dagmar wasn't my only Amish friend. I've got plenty of Amish friends. You marry young, except for Dagmar. She chose to remain a single person. In my day they called them spinsters. Left on the shelf—passed by."

"I shall be like Dagmar and never marry."

"That's best. Most of them are no good. Not much point to them, except for working on the farm."

"And do any of your Amish friends know who this girl is?"

"I do have a name."

"You have a first name?"

"I do. And a last name, too."

Cherish cleared her throat. "Would it be Annie Whiley?"

"How did you know?"

"It wasn't too hard to figure out. She's the only girl around here close to his age. Do you think they're more than friends?"

"As I said, I see the buggy there all the time. How long are you staying for?"

"A couple of days."

"If she doesn't visit while you're there, I'd say it's more than likely that they're boyfriend and girlfriend and they don't want to go public yet, or something worse." Ruth smiled and winked at her. "Could be up to no good."

"Oh no, I don't think anything like that would be going on, not on my farm."

"Like I said, if you find out anything, let me know first."

"Yes, I will, Ruth. Just as long as you let me know whatever you find out, or tell me whatever you see."

"We have a deal." Ruth smiled, reached out her hand over the table to Cherish, and they shook on it.

CHAPTER NINETEEN

*C*herish walked back to the farm, stewing on the information Ruth had given her. It didn't sit well with her having Annie Whiley at the farm when she wasn't there. She couldn't control his personal life, but she hoped he wasn't behaving inappropriately.

When she got back to the house, she saw Carter in one of the fields quite far away. Then she walked in to see Florence sitting in the living room.

"Ah, you're back. Did you have a nice talk with Ruth?"

"I did." She slumped into the couch next to Florence. "It won't be long before I can take over and he doesn't need to act all high and mighty toward me. He's just rude most of the time."

"I think he's been doing a pretty good job. The place is almost spotless." Florence frowned and pointed to the kitchen.

Cherish grimaced guessing Malachi was in there and that meant he'd probably overheard her. She'd assumed he'd be somewhere out in the fields with Carter, not staying with the women in the house. *"Jah, well, that's what I expected."* Cherish walked into the kitchen and saw Malachi sitting down with a mug of coffee. "Oh, I thought you were out in the field, working. Shouldn't you be? I thought I saw you there."

"No. You might have seen Carter. He went for a walk."

Even though she had meant every word, she hoped he hadn't heard what she'd said about him. Looking at his mug, she asked, "Where's mine?"

He jumped up. "I'll get you one now."

Cherish grunted. "Don't worry, I'll get my own. I can see if anything's going to get done around here I'll have to do it."

"Aren't you happy with my work?"

Florence walked into the room before Cherish had a chance to answer. "Yes, we are. More than happy. Has anyone seen Carter?"

"He's gone for a walk, it seems." Cherish picked up the kettle. "Florence, would you like a cup of coffee?"

"No, I'm fine."

Cherish promptly placed the kettle down and ran past Florence and continued out of the house. The last thing she wanted was for Malachi to see her cry and if she stayed in the room any longer that would've happened.

All of a sudden, a hand grabbed her on the shoulder and she spun around to see Florence.

"What's upset you now?"

Cherish sniffed and wiped her eyes as she looked past Florence back to the house. She wanted to make certain that Malachi couldn't see her. "Don't say that. It sounds like I'm always upset if you say that and I'm not."

"I'm sorry. What's wrong?"

"Some things upset me, certain people upset me when they do certain things."

"I'm guessing we're talking about Malachi. What's he done now?"

"You know. He's gone and changed everything."

"I know, but they're good changes. And sometimes certain things should be changed to make them better, not worse. Don't you think what he's done is for the best?"

"No, I do not think the changes are for the best. I think they are for the worst, because when I'm old enough to take over the farm, things would've changed completely." Cherish gasped for air. She knew she wasn't really upset about the changes on the farm.

She hated her life!

Dat was gone, *Mamm* was unkind, and Florence had abandoned them.

Cherish took a deep breath. "And then when I take over the place, I won't know what to do and then I'll have to ask him to show me what to do." Another tear trickled down Cherish's cheek.

"What would that matter?" Florence rubbed her shoulder and smiled reassuringly. "You're upsetting yourself over nothing."

"I don't like having to ask people for help."

"You mean you don't like having to ask *people* for help, or you don't want to have to ask *him* for help?"

Cherish sniffed and wiped her eyes.

"Let's sit down over here." Florence led her to an old wooden seat under a tree. The same bench where she'd talked with Malachi earlier.

She sat down next to Florence. "I just don't like things that change—do you?"

"Life changes, everything in life changes. You're right, though, I don't like it sometimes. Nothing ever stays the same."

Cherish huffed. "Now you're sounding like *him.*"

"I'm not meaning to sound like anybody, but it's true."

"Why did Dagmar have to die? It's so unfair. It's sad to be here when she's not. We're using her things, being in her house. When he changes things, I feel I'm losing more of her." She did her best to blink back the tears.

Florence put both arms around Cherish and let her little sister cry onto her shoulder. "I understand. I understand perfectly. I feel the same about *Dat's* orchard."

"You do?"

"I do. It feels awful knowing Levi is going to make changes that I know will ruin all my hard work. At least Malachi is making changes for the good of the farm."

Cherish sniffled. Florence did have a point. All the Baker girls knew it was a disaster having Levi run the orchard.

Florence continued, "They'll be harvesting any day and you've got out of all that hard work."

Cherish giggled and felt better. "I did, didn't I?"

"Yes. Before we go tomorrow morning, I want you to give Malachi some words of encouragement. He's a good man and he's doing his best."

"Okay."

"Besides," Florence whispered. "If he goes, we might not be able to find anyone else."

Cherish wiped her eyes. "I might as well talk to him now. Then I'll think about cooking the dinner."

"Good girl. And I'll find Carter."

Cherish walked back to the house and nearly bumped into Malachi as he was coming out. They stood at the front door, face-to-face. "Can we talk?" she asked in a small voice.

"Sure. Go on."

She looked over her shoulder at Florence walking away. "Let's sit." She walked over to one of the porch chairs and sat.

He hesitated and then sat on the one next to her. "Look. I can explain. It only happened the one time."

Cherish frowned at him and played along. "I'm surprised it happened at all."

"I know." He looked down.

"Well, explain."

He laughed. "I'm joking with you."

Cherish growled. "You're so annoying!" She quickly reminded herself to be nice. "What I want to say is you're doing an okay job around here."

"You mean it? For real?"

"Yes and … and thank … you." The words stuck in her throat.

He leaned back in the chair. "For a second there I thought I'd be packin' me things."

"Not for a while, but don't get too comfortable."

"I won't."

"Now, I'll go inside and see what I can rustle up for dinner."

"Saves me cookin.' I'm a pretty good cook, but now you're doin' it, I can get more work in while it's daylight."

"Good. Off you go, then."

He rose to his feet and glanced back at her and smiled, before he took a giant leap off the porch with his long legs, missing the steps entirely. She was glad she'd come and put her fears to rest.

On the drive home early the next day, Cherish was careful not to talk too much.

"Thanks for helping me out, both of you."

"You're welcome." Carter glanced at her in the rear-view mirror and smiled.

"Can I have your sewing machine, Florence?"

"No. I've been meaning to get it. It was my mother's."

"I know it was, I've heard that six thousand and twenty-five times. But since you left it, I thought you might not want it any more. What use would it be now to you? Aren't you wearing store-bought clothes?"

"I still like to sew. It's calming and helps me to relax."

Cherish sighed. "I'll have Joy get Isaac to bring it to you. He won't mind. He'll do anything she asks."

Florence laughed. "Okay, thanks. We could collect it in the car, but I don't think Wilma would like that too much."

"No, she wouldn't."

"Have you heard when she's getting married yet?"

"I heard it was in the middle of December sometime."

"Ah, that's what I heard too. It'll be quite different around the place for you when Bliss and Levi move in." Florence wondered how her father would feel about Wilma living there with a new husband.

"I won't be there long enough for it to worry me."

"Where are you going?" Carter asked.

"I plan to move to the farm as soon as I possibly can. As soon as I'm old enough, or the moment *Mamm* allows me."

"Perhaps you might see that running the farm is not as easy as you think." Carter said.

Florence knew right away he'd said the wrong thing.

"I stayed for several months with Aunt Dagmar, and I know exactly what to do. She showed me everything. She must've known, I mean, she did know that she was going to leave it to me and that's why she made sure that she showed me everything. I just thought she was doing it to be educational, but she was doing it because I was going to take over. And take over I will."

"I'm sure you'll do a good job," Carter said.

"Thank you. Nice that someone thinks so. I don't mind making changes once I'm in charge. It's not as though I'm against changes. It's just that I want everything to stay the same until I get there, because I know what to do with everything as it is."

"I can quite understand," Carter said. "I'm glad everything ended well and you and Malachi could make some kind of truce."

"I was never fighting with him. It was never an argument. Not when I was his boss telling him what to do."

"I think we should have some music now, don't you?"

Carter turned on some music and it wasn't long before Cherish fell asleep.

CHAPTER TWENTY

*I*t was now days after Florence and Carter returned from Cherish's farm, and the harvest next door still hadn't begun.

Florence walked into the house after being out to get a closer look at her former trees. Heartbroken, she closed the door behind her and when she heard Carter in the kitchen, she walked in and sat down. Carter was busily cutting up vegetables. He'd become a little interested in cooking just like he'd said he might.

He looked across at her. "What's wrong? You look like you've got the weight of the world on your shoulders."

"They should've harvested before now. *Well* before now." She bit the side of her lip. "I think they're going by the date we did the harvest last year, but they can't go by dates alone. Last year the weather was different. They have to go by the trees—by the fruit. They have to read the signs."

"I know there's no good saying this to you, but I will anyway. The problem is not yours to worry about. Forget about next door and concentrate on what we've got going on with our orchard."

"I know, but I still feel like it's my orchard, and their failure feels like my failure." She looked up at him expecting another lecture, but all he did was smile. "What are we having for dinner tonight?"

"Nothing too fancy. You'll have to wait and see."

"Need any help? It'll keep my mind off what's happening next door."

"Concentrate on us. You, me, and the children that will come along, whenever they decide to. They'll help us run the orchard and you can teach them everything you know about apple trees."

She giggled. "I can't wait for that."

"It's something we can look forward to when it happens."

She knew everything Carter said was right. It was useless worrying about what they were doing next door but it was hard not to. And what were the girls doing? Why weren't they helping Levi? She'd taught them to watch for the signs of when the fruit was ready. Maybe they had told Levi, and he just wasn't listening.

"What is it now?" He placed his sharp-bladed knife down.

"I'm just thinking the girls must know the harvest should've been done days ago."

"What do you want to do? Do you want to go over there and tell him that they've made a mistake?"

Florence shook her head. "No, that wouldn't be good. Wilma wouldn't want to know she's made a mistake. She thinks Levi is wonderful even though he hasn't done a thing to deserve her adoration. It's simply by default. I've gone and she needs to rely on someone."

"There's your answer, then."

She stared at him. "What's my answer?"

He picked up the knife and started chopping again. "If you can't do anything about it, or you're not willing to do anything about it, why worry?"

Carter had the same easy-going nature as her father. She slowly nodded and reminded herself to relax more. It wasn't possible to have control over everything. "I'll fix myself a cup of tea. Want one?"

"Not for me, thanks," he said.

She rose to her feet and then filled up the teakettle and flicked on the electrical switch, and then she folded her arms and stared out the window.

What would her father think of everything that was going on next door?

He'd be happy she was living in the old place, in the cottage where their visitors used to stay. It'd hurt him to sell it; she remembered that vividly. He'd had little choice since they'd had five bad harvests in a row. With Wilma adding six more children heading to adulthood, there were many mouths to feed. It had been her father's long-term plan to leave land around the cottage and plant the rest.

"Carter, when I was young, I was certain there was another house near this one."

"On the same land?"

"Yes."

"The people I bought the place from told me there was a smaller building. They showed me the stone foundations."

"I'm pleased I'm not losing my mind. One of the girls mentioned it too, once, or I might've clean forgotten about it. We played in it many years ago. What happened to it?"

"Burned to the ground, they said. It happened before they bought the place."

"I don't remember it happening. Wasn't it built from stone, so how did it burn?"

"That's what they told me. It probably had a wooden frame, not sure. The old owners walked me around the property the day before the papers were finalized. I stubbed my foot on a rock and then they moved the grass and showed me where the old foundations were. It was only as big as one room."

"Whereabouts is it?"

"Near the cherry tree. I'll show you tomorrow."

"Thanks. I'd like to see it."

"It should bring back a few childhood memories by the sound of it."

"I think so. I had fun with the girls when they were little." Florence stared out the window once more.

Carter's chuckling startled her, and she turned around. "What's funny?"

"I was just thinking, here you are with me in the kitchen. I used to spend a lot of time gazing out this window or the living room window hoping to catch a glimpse of you. Hoping you'd come down by the fence to tell me off about the cows or to tell me something—anything. I used to wait for your evening walks hoping you'd come close to the fence."

She couldn't help smiling. "Did you?"

"I did. I spent a lot of time waiting, looking out windows. And here you are now, with me as my wife. I can't ask for anything more than that. It was as though someone had planned everything."

"Aha, but you don't believe in God."

"That's right, I said, 'as though,' and I never mentioned God. Don't go putting words into my mouth. If there was a God, he might have designed the whole thing. Was it God, or was it fate? Who knows?"

"Why do you have to choose? Can't it be both?" She knew that God would've put it into place, and that was what fate was.

He shook his head and went back to chopping the vegeta-

165

bles. "Whatever it was that made you fall in love with me, I'm grateful."

"Me too."

He popped the vegetables into the saucepan, wiped his hands on a paper towel and then walked over to the window to stand next to her. Once he had put his arm around her, he asked, "How soon will it be before this place is flowering with apple trees?"

"It won't be next year. It won't be the year after, either."

"Six years?"

"I'd say six, yes, most likely."

"I'm looking forward to it."

"Me too."

"I never thought I'd like living in the country. I like being away from the hustle and bustle."

As she watched Spot rolling in the grass, she knew that leaving the orchard was a small price to pay for being with the man she loved. It wasn't just the orchard she had left, it was her whole way of life she'd left to be with Carter. "I'm sorry I've been so hard to live with over the last few days. I almost wanted to get in there and pick them myself."

"Why don't we offer to help them?"

Was he serious? She turned to look into his face. "You'd do that?"

"I would if they could use our help."

"That wouldn't be a good idea. Wilma would see it as some kind of attack on her as though she doesn't know what she's doing or something."

"Ah yes, I can see why she would probably think that."

"I might take Spot for a walk."

"Another walk?" He looked out the window at Spot who was now walking toward the house.

"Yes. A quick one."

"Okay, but keep your eyes to the right, don't even look next door or you'll only get upset again."

"I know. I'll try not to." She gave him a quick kiss on his cheek and headed out of the house, grabbing the leash by the front door as she went.

Spot picked up his pace when he saw her.

"Come on, Spot." He ran faster when she held up the lead. He loved his walks. He sat down, quivering with excitement while she clipped his leash onto his collar.

As they walked, Spot looked up into the distance. Even though she was trying not to take any notice of what was happening on the Baker side of the fence, she had to see what Spot was looking at so intently.

It was Favor, and she was waving her hands over her head.

Florence stopped still in shock, and then she walked over to meet her.

CHAPTER TWENTY-ONE

They met at the fence line. "Hello, Favor."

"Hello, I've got some papers for you, and some good news."

"Finally, someone's brought my mother's papers. Is that what they are?"

"Jah. Cherish went up and got them."

"Thank you." Florence took hold of them. "What is the good news? Is Levi starting the harvest tomorrow? I hope that's the good news because it's long overdue."

"It's not about the orchard. It's about Honor and Mercy—they're both pregnant!"

"Really? Both of them?"

"Jah."

Favor jumped up and down with excitement causing Spot to bark at her.

Florence patted Spot to quiet him. "I'm so pleased for them. It's fantastic news."

"They're both really happy, and the *bopplis* are due about the same time." Favor giggled loudly. "You know how competitive they are? Now they're in a race to see which one comes first."

"You mean, which baby is born first?"

Favor nodded.

Florence laughed. "This is so good for Mercy. She was so sad over losing her first child, and nothing will make up for that, but I'm sure she's overjoyed she's having another."

"She is."

She looked back at Favor. It felt like she hadn't seen her for years. "And look at you. You've gotten so tall."

"Have I?" Favor looked down to her feet and looked back up again and stretched herself up on her tiptoes.

Florence laughed.

"I'm the same height as *Mamm* now."

"I think you'll be the tallest of all the girls."

"I hope I am going to be as tall as you, Florence. I want to be tall."

"I think you might be." Florence couldn't help trying to get a look at the low branches of the trees, heavy with fruit, over Favor's shoulder. "What's happening with the orchard?"

"We're picking the fruit the day after tomorrow."

"That's not ideal."

"Joy told Levi that, but he arranged to do it months ago on the same date we did it last year."

"I knew it," Florence spat out before she could stop herself. "I knew that's what he was doing. It should've been done by now."

Favor nodded. "I don't know why *Mamm's* listening to him. He's hardly been at the orchard at all. It's just wasting away. I'm really worried and I'm not the only one. He's not even opening the shop this year."

"Why not?"

"He said *Mamm* had enough to do. She explained you used to run the shop, and we used to do the roadside stalls since we closed the market stall."

"It doesn't sound like anyone's doing anything."

Favor shrugged her shoulders. Of course the girls wouldn't be too worried about having less work—they were too young to truly realize the consequences.

"Mamm's not worried?"

"Nee, not about that."

Florence could see from Favor's face there was something else. "What is she worried about?"

"Levi hasn't set a date for the wedding yet."

171

Florence's eyebrows shot up. "Are they getting married, or not?"

Favor leaned forward. "Well ... I think that's what *Mamm's* worried about."

"I thought he was crazy-madly in love with her."

"I don't know. It seems as soon as she said she'd marry him, he's not been around there so much."

"And she's giving him the orchard to run? It doesn't make sense." Florence bit down on the inside of her mouth trying to stop herself from getting too upset.

"She's in love with him, and I suppose she wants to do everything he says. Especially now you've left, he's the only person she can turn to." Favor crouched down, put her arm through the fence and patted Spot.

"When are Joy and Isaac getting married, then?"

"Beginning of December. I'm not sure what date. Are you coming to the wedding?"

"If I can, I will. I don't want to miss seeing her get married, but if it's too difficult for everybody, I won't come."

"I hope you come. Do you like being married?"

"I do, I like being married to Carter, I'll put it that way. I don't know if I would like being married to anybody else."

Favor giggled. "That's funny."

There were so many other things Florence wanted to ask her, like who was sewing Joy's dress for the wedding.

She'd always done the sewing for the family. That reminded her about her mother's treadle sewing machine. It was still at the house. It was no good mentioning it to Favor. She'd have to face Wilma one day and ask for it.

"Tell Carter I said hello."

"I will." Florence stood there clutching her mother's paperwork, wondering if she'd ever get to hold her nieces or nephews. "Thank you for telling me the good news and for this." She held up the papers.

"*Jah,* sure. I should get home. Bye, Florence."

"Bye, Favor."

Favor gave her a big smile, turned and walked away.

WHEN SHE WALKED up to the house she told Carter the news about the coming babies. He was more interested in seeing the paperwork. "My mother's name was Jones. Eleanor Jones."

"Now you know. Can I see?"

She handed them over and he walked off with them and sat down next to his laptop.

"What are you going to do with them?"

"I'm going to take pictures and send them to the investigator who located Wilma."

"Thank you."

He took out his cell phone and photographed each page of

the paperwork. Her mother's birth certificate from the hospital and another one—the official one from the county—and her wedding certificate. "With all this, we'll find one of your relatives in no time. If there are any out there."

She sat down next to him and watched what he was doing; desperately hoping she'd find someone connected to her mother.

CHAPTER TWENTY-TWO

*T*hat night, Florence and Carter were just about to sit down to an early dinner when they heard a buggy.

Florence opened the front door. "It's Christina," she told Carter.

"I'll put our dinners in the oven. I'll be upstairs."

"Okay." She walked out and then Christina jumped down and threw her horse's reins over the hitching post.

"Christina, is everything alright?"

Christina rushed to her. "Have you heard the news?"

"About what?"

"Honor and Mercy."

"I have. It's such good news for them."

"Good news for them, but not for me. Why haven't I had a baby yet, Florence? Why do I keep missing out?"

Florence guessed dinner wasn't going to be for quite a while. "I don't know. Would you like to come inside and have some dinner with us?"

"Oh, I'm so selfish. I've called at a bad time, haven't I? I've called at your mealtime. It's early to have dinner. I've got mine made already, but Mark's not even home yet."

"It doesn't matter, I thought you might like to have some with us."

"No, but I won't hold you up. Would you visit with me tomorrow?"

"Yes, I would like that very much, but we can talk now if you want."

"I'd rather see you tomorrow. Shall we say ... eleven?"

"Perfect. I'm sure Carter will be able to drive me to your place."

"I could come and collect you?"

"No, that should be fine."

She leaned forward and hugged Florence. "I'll see you tomorrow, and I'll try not to talk about what's happened. There's no use moaning about things that I can't change, but I would like to see you."

"And I would like to see you, too."

The two women laughed and then parted. Florence got to the front door and looked around to see that Christina was already driving off. She closed the door and walked back to the kitchen and sat down.

"That was fast," Carter said as he walked down the stairs. "Stay there. I'll get your dinner out of the oven." He brought their dinners back and sat them down on the table. "What did she want?"

"She heard the news about Honor and Mercy. She was a little upset."

"Ah, yes you told me about that. Her not being able to have children."

"Well she did once, so that means it's possible that she will again."

"Anything is possible, but somethings aren't probable especially when the doctor tells her so."

"But still it must be sad for her to see other people getting pregnant around her." She put her fork into a piece of potato and looked up at Carter. "The funny thing is, Christina and I never really got along and now we're getting along much better since I've left."

"What do you think that means?" he asked.

"She was always difficult to get along with. I think it was Wilma who was the problem. Christina never forgave her for giving her bad advice about adopting her baby out. Maybe there was more, too. More that Christina's not saying."

"Wilma shouldn't have interfered in something like that. I can fully understand why Christina's upset about that. And I think Wilma had an ulterior motive as well."

"What motive could she have possibly had?"

"You told me how she's always worried about what people think. People might have thought that the baby was Mark's and that they had to get married because she was pregnant. Wouldn't that look bad for Mark?"

"I never thought of that. Yes, it would. And, being bad for Mark would mean looking bad for Wilma and the whole family." Florence shook her head. "I would hate to think that's true of Wilma."

"I've seen people do a lot of strange things in my time, and Wilma is a little odd. I didn't want anything from her; I just wanted to get to know her. Well, I guess I am getting to know her from her actions rather than her words. She's nothing like Iris. *She* was my real mother."

"I wish I had met her, and your father. They sound like lovely people."

"They were the best. I wish you could've got to meet them too. They would've loved you just as much as I love you."

Florence giggled. "That would've been nice."

"I hope Christina doesn't want to cry on your shoulder tomorrow. You've had enough of petty dramas."

It was more than petty dramas in this case. "Christina's not like that. She's got deep hurts. She did say she was going to try not to speak about that and the despair she feels, but I don't mind if she does. Everybody needs to vent every now and again. I do it myself sometimes."

His eyebrows rose. "You don't vent to me. I know when you're upset though. If you don't talk to me, with whom do you talk?"

"Spot. He's a good listener. And, he never argues or disagrees. He's the perfect friend."

They both laughed.

CHAPTER TWENTY-THREE

*T*he next day Carter took Florence to Christina's.

"Shall I collect you in an hour?" he asked as she got out of the car. "That'll give me time to do a few things."

"I think so. If I'm ready earlier I'll call you." When Carter drove away, she walked up to the door and knocked on it.

Christina answered the door with a smile.

"This is a surprise," Florence said as she greeted Christina with a hug.

"What is?"

"You're smiling. I was sure you were going to be depressed."

"Nee, I'm pleased. This morning I got a large order for prayer *kapps."*

"Oh good. I'm glad to hear it. How large is it?"

"Large enough to keep me busy and keep my mind occupied so I don't think about other things."

"That is a blessing."

"It is. It's a huge blessing. That's exactly what Mark said when I called him up to tell him about it."

They sat down on the couch in front of a tray of tea items Christina had ready.

"This all looks good. I asked Carter to pick me up in an hour, will that be okay?"

"Perfect."

"That way I won't keep you from making all your prayer *kapps*."

Christina gave a little giggle.

"What else is going on in your world?" asked Florence as Christina poured the tea.

"Isaac has arranged with Wilma for him and Joy to live there after they're married. Can you believe it?"

"I guess I can. It makes sense. The house is plenty big enough, anyway."

Christina scowled. "Don't you start."

"Start what?"

"Everyone's talking about this place being too small, but it suits us just fine even with Isaac staying here."

Florence knew the house was small no matter what Christina thought. "Well it would be too small for them both to live here once they're married, don't you think?"

"I do." Christina handed Florence a cup of tea.

"Thank you." Florence took a sip, then set it down.

"It's too small for two couples but it's not too small for a couple and one child. When the business goes better we can buy a bigger *haus* or build onto this one."

"That sounds like a good idea."

"That's what I would want if we had *kinner.*"

Florence hadn't wanted the conversation to go there. "Well, it sounds like Joy and Isaac are making sensible plans. What about Wilma and Levi?"

"They're getting married a few days after Joy, can you believe it?"

"No, I can't. There are many things I don't want to believe. I was talking to Favor and she said a date for Wilma and Levi's wedding hasn't been made."

"It's only just been decided. I don't think Wilma's even told the girls yet."

"I see."

"Wilma's upset with Joy because Wilma suggested they have a combined wedding. Joy didn't want to and Wilma's most upset about that. So, they're having their wedding a few days after Joy and Isaac's."

"She's not been getting on too well with the girls, then?" Florence inquired already knowing the answer.

"That's right. Everything fell apart when you left."

Florence sipped on her tea feeling dreadfully guilty, but deep down she was satisfied that she was missed.

"Just a minute, I wrote it down." Christina jumped up and grabbed a sheet of paper from the bureau under the window.

"Wrote what down?"

Christina continued, "December seven is when Isaac and Joy are getting married and December fifteen is when Wilma and Levi are getting married." She tossed the paper back on the bureau and sat back down on the couch.

"That is a surprise."

"It's good that you got away from them. Honor is the only sensible one out of the lot of them."

"What about Joy?"

Christina smiled. "She's not normal. She's far too serious and superior if you want my opinion, which you did because you just asked. I like her and everything. Maybe she'll grow out of it when she's older."

"Perhaps. I think Isaac has been a good influence for her already." Florence had another sip of tea and wondered how much time had passed. She was already missing being near Carter.

CHAPTER TWENTY-FOUR

*L*ater that day, after Florence's afternoon stroll, she stepped into the house, leaned down and unclipped Spot's leash. Spot ran and sat on one of the couches just as she hung up the leash by the front door.

Carter walked downstairs and she looked over at him. "What do you look so happy about?"

"I have a surprise for you."

Florence saw he was hiding something behind his back just as he had done on their wedding day when he produced the wedding rings. "I told you I don't need an engagement ring."

He laughed. "It's not about an engagement ring. It's something quite different."

He was smiling, so it couldn't be anything bad. "Do I have to sit down for this?"

"Perhaps."

"You haven't bought another orchard without telling me about it, have you?"

"No. I promised to tell you, next time."

When she sat on the couch, he sat down next to her and took hold of both her hands. Then she saw the papers he'd placed on the other side of him. "It's about your mother's family," he said, his expression a mix of excitement and nerves.

"You found someone?" By his attitude, she knew he wasn't going to say they were all dead.

"Yes. Your mother's mother."

She couldn't believe it. "I have a grandmother, still living?"

"You do. She hasn't seen her daughter since Eleanor was nineteen. She had no idea whether she was alive or dead."

"That's awful. She knows now?"

"She does. Eleanor left her family, and after years had gone by, they thought the worst."

Florence sighed. "Oh. That's terrible."

"There were tragedies within the family. Turns out, her older brother was in jail for murdering his father, your grandfather."

"I have an uncle who's a murderer?" She put her hands to her head. "This is a lot to take in." Then she looked over at him. "Why are you so happy if this is the news?"

"Because my friend found out that your grandmother wants to see you."

"She does?"

He nodded enthusiastically. "Yes, she does."

"She's been told about me?" Her hand rested on her throat.

"That's right."

"I can't believe it. Does she know about Earl and Mark?"

"No. Perhaps you can tell her that yourself when you meet her."

"When?"

"Tomorrow."

Florence gulped, wide-eyed with shock. "So soon?"

"If you want."

"Yes, yes. Where does she live?"

"A couple hours' drive, in Baltimore."

"I can't wait to talk with her and find out everything about my mother. Do you know why my uncle murdered my grandfather?"

"I did some research and the son claims he ran him down by accident."

"Ran over him in a car?"

"That's right. In the driveway of the family home. Your grandfather got out of the car when your uncle was

SAMANTHA PRICE

taking him home. Your uncle said he assumed he would walk towards the house in front of the car, but for some reason he walked behind the car."

"Oh, that's terrible. And no one believed it was an accident?"

"Apparently not, for various reasons. I haven't looked into the full details of it yet, but I will."

"What a tragedy."

"Your mother didn't stick around for the investigation. She ran off and they never saw her again."

"I wonder what happened between her leaving and her joining the Amish community. I wonder where she met my father. I must fill in the missing pieces."

He shook his head. "It might not be possible to know everything. Since your father died and no one else seems to know anything about her. You said everyone's remained closed-lipped where she's concerned."

"Yes. I haven't talked to the bishop about her yet. Surely, he would be the one to know some things."

"Quite possibly. Talk to your grandmother first, and see what she can tell you."

She wrapped her arms around Carter's neck. "Thank you, thank you so much. This means everything. Now I can learn about my mother, find out what she was like. I wonder where she got the treadle sewing machine. I always assumed it was passed down from her mother, but now I know that's not likely. When she ran away, she wouldn't have taken it with her."

"You'll soon find out. You'll soon have pieces to your puzzle just like I found pieces to mine."

"Thank you, Carter." She wrapped her arms around his neck.

MEANWHILE AT THE BAKER HOME, Cherish looked at the few chickens they kept and giggled as she thought about Malachi. On her next visit, she had to help him overcome his fears. A farmer scared of a harmless chicken just wasn't right. It wasn't too early to plan her next visit to the farm. She'd bring along a few surprises.

First there's Joy's wedding, and then Wilma's—and won't that one be fun? she thought sarcastically, gritting her teeth. She didn't see herself living at home for much longer. Her farm was the key. It was the key to her escape. She was ready to embrace life's changes and challenges.

"*Denke, Gott*, and Aunt Dagmar," Cherish murmured before she headed to the house to write another letter to her caretaker.

CHAPTER TWENTY-FIVE

*T*he staff at the old-people's home where Betty Jones lived knew Betty was being introduced to her granddaughter today. They were there to greet Florence and Carter when they arrived, and they took her to Betty's room while Carter stayed in the reception area.

On the way there, the nurse told her, "She's not doing well, so don't expect her to show any recognition."

"It'll be all right to tell her who I am?"

"Yes, but she might not respond. This way."

Florence left Carter in the reception area and walked with the nurse.

"This is her room." The nurse pushed the door open and then went in first.

Florence walked in behind her to see a small white-haired woman in a bed. It could've been anyone's grandmother, but this one was hers.

The woman looked up and stared at her. A faint smile hinted around her lips. "Eleanor."

Florence looked over at the nurse wondering what to do. The nurse shrugged her shoulders. Looking back at Betty, she said, "I'm Eleanor's daughter, Florence."

"Her daughter?"

"I am."

"That's right. They told me about you. Come closer." Florence walked over to her bed. Betty said, "You look just like her. What's your name?"

"Florence." The woman reached her hand to her and Florence took hold of it and held onto it.

Florence felt connected right away. In her mind, she tried to figure out what Betty would've looked like in her youth.

"You look exactly the same as her but perhaps you're a little bit taller, I think. It's hard to tell from the bed."

"I'm pleased I look like her. I don't remember her much. She died when I was two."

"They told me that. They said she went to live with the Amish. I wish she would've told me, or contacted me. Would you like my photos?"

"I would love to see photos."

"You can have them all. I'll keep one or two. I'll be gone soon and no one will want them."

The nurse brought a box from the other side of the room and set it on the end of the bed.

"Take a look in the box."

Florence moved to the end of the bed, opened the box and then pulled out a framed photograph. She turned it toward Betty. "Is this my mother?"

"It is."

It was like seeing a photograph of herself. "There were no photos of her. This is the first time I've seen her. I saw her as a baby, of course. Our community does not allow photographs to be taken. I've always wanted to see her." Tears rolled down her face and she wiped them away. "Ohh, I told myself not to cry." The only difference Florence saw was her mother's hair was curly, while her own was straight. "She was a teenager here?"

"That's right."

"She had such curly hair."

"That wasn't her natural hair. Hers was just like yours. Bring the box closer and I'll show them to you."

One by one Betty showed her photographs and told her who was who. She saw more photos of her mother, and her uncle, and many of Betty and Betty's husband, her grandfather.

"When they told me that Eleanor had had a child, I just couldn't believe it.

"It's true. Here I am."

"They told me she ran away to join the Amish, is that right?"

"It is. I was raised Amish and I only recently left them. She died when I was two and I barely remember anything about her. I always assumed she'd grown up in the community. I was surprised to learn she hadn't."

"Tell me about your life."

"I have two older brothers. They're Eleanor's children too. Our father was a wonderful man. We had an apple orchard."

Her eyes grew wide. "An apple orchard you say?"

"That's right."

"Maybe she met him during fruit picking."

Florence never knew how they met. "It's quite possible. We do, I mean, we did employ people outside of the community for the yearly harvest. It would be interesting to know if that's how they met. I just got married."

"Ah, that's nice for you."

"It is."

"She's doing well today," the nurse said. "You got her on one of her good days."

"Don't listen to her," Betty said with a grin.

Florence giggled, and didn't know what to say, so she turned her attention back to the photos. "I can't believe it. I was hoping you would have one photograph, I never imagined you might have all these."

"I'll sort out some that you can take before you go."

"Really?" Florence stared at them. At last, she'd see her mother.

"Yes."

"I would love that. Thank you."

When they finished looking at the photographs and Betty had sorted out ones Florence could take, Betty stared into her face. "And what is it you do?"

"I grew up on the apple orchard, so that's what I do. I've left my father's orchard because his Amish wife—my stepmother—now has that, and I live next door. My new husband and I are starting an orchard from the ground up. It's quite exciting."

"New husband and new orchard. Both will grow together."

"That's right, they will." It felt good to Florence to say, 'my husband,' words she never thought she would utter.

"They have teacake here," Betty said.

"Oh, that sounds nice."

"Sometimes with raisins. And where is your husband?"

"He's here waiting for me."

"You left him in the car?"

"He's in the building."

"Bring him in right now. I must meet him."

"Okay."

The nurse smiled. "I'll fetch him, and I might see if we can find some of that teacake for you and your guests, Betty."

Betty's face beamed. "We'd like that." When the nurse left, Betty said, "Thank goodness she's gone. Why does she have to stand there and listen to everything? Do they think I'm plotting an escape? I would, but I can't run very fast. They'd catch up with me."

Florence smiled at her.

"They think I'm going senile, but I'm not. I always forget things, have done for years. Still, they look after me and the food's good."

"That's the main thing. How are you doing? Do you need anything at all."

"No. I'm fine. I can't complain. I've got friends here. Did Eleanor have a good life?"

"She did. She loved me and my brothers very much, and our father. He was a lovely man, quiet and patient."

"I'm pleased to hear it. I had to tell myself she'd died, when she hadn't returned for years. That was the only way I could cope. Turns out she *had* died. I just wish I had known."

Florence moved closer to her. "Seems like we were both looking for answers."

Carter walked into the room alone, with no nurse in sight. Florence introduced them.

"You've made my wife very happy, Betty."

"And she has made me very happy. We figured out that Eleanor must've met her Amish husband while she was doing fruit picking. Isn't that right, Florence?"

"There's a good chance that's how they met. I hope there's some way I can find out. I'm thinking to ask the bishop, but I haven't seen him since I've left. So that would be awkward."

"Well if you find anything out, I'd love to know. You will keep in touch with me, won't you, Florence?"

"I'd love to."

"And your uncle is innocent. I suppose someone told you about him, so I want you to know that."

Florence nodded. "Thanks for telling me."

The nurse came back into the room a few minutes later with hot tea and teacake.

DRIVING AWAY from where her grandmother lived, a light smattering of rain fell from the sky. The automated windshield wipers started their job.

Florence turned to her husband. "Thank you, Carter. That's the best thing you've ever done for me. I never thought I would meet my grandmother and now I've got all these photos of my mother. I feel I know her now. What a brave woman she was to run away, leaving her family and picking fruit just to get by."

"She sounds like she was a very gutsy lady. And then she met your father and fell in love."

"That's right. I can't wait to tell Earl and Mark about our grandmother. They might want to visit her. I hope they do. I want to come back and see her soon, too."

"Anytime you want."

Florence's thoughts turned back to the letter her mother left her. Then it dawned on her what the mistake was— the one that she said she didn't want Florence to repeat. "Do you remember the letter I showed you from my mother?"

"Of course I do. You look at it every day."

"That's right. I know what the mistake was now."

"What was it?" he asked giving her another quick sideways glance.

"She said in her letter for me not to make the same mistake that she did. She left her family and didn't keep in touch."

He swallowed hard. "You have a very different family compared to the one she had."

"It doesn't matter. Family is family. I know you feel rejected by Wilma and you feel like cutting her and everybody else off, but I've grown up very close to my sisters— and yours—and they'll always be my family. Wilma raised me and did the best she could. She loved me, she did."

"You said she treated you differently."

"I only noticed that when I was older. I didn't notice that when I was growing up. She was a loving mother back then and it can't have been easy raising three stepchildren and six of her own."

Carter glanced at her, taking his eyes off the road for an instant. "Maybe not but, by the sounds of it, you were there to help her every step of the way."

"I was, but I'm not going to cut them off completely."

"You must do what makes you comfortable. I'm happy with whatever you decide. I feel no connection, you're right about that, just as Wilma feels no connection with me. Even though I am related to Wilma and the girls, for me, that's where it ends."

Florence knew in her heart that he would've felt different if Wilma had opened her heart to him. Now he had built walls around himself in regard to Wilma and the rest of them. "I'm just pleased now that I know what my mother was talking about in her letter."

"Me too."

"Are you sure?"

He glanced over at her once more. "Positive. I like to see you smile."

"I'm always smiling, aren't I?"

"Not when you're worried about those bonnet sisters of yours."

She ignored the reference to her half-sisters, and looked out the window at the rain.

"The Jenkins have cleared their things out of the cottage."

"Cottage? Oh, yes, there's a cottage there. I've seen it from the road."

"Let's have a look at it."

"Right now?"

"Yes. They aren't using it and we could lease it out for extra income. The Jenkins only need the house, they said."

Florence tapped her fingers on her chin. "I know the perfect couple who could move into the cottage."

He stopped at an intersection and stared at her from under his thick dark lashes. "I'm afraid to ask."

"Joy and Isaac after they get married. Maybe Isaac could move in there now and do any repairs that need to be done and get it ready for when they get married. Christina told me he planned to ask Wilma if he and Joy could live in the family home after their wedding, but I have to believe it would be better for them to have their own place."

He chuckled. "We haven't even seen it ourselves yet. Let's just take one step at a time. Besides, do you have any idea whether your Amish bishop will allow them to stay in a place that we own? And let's not get started on what Wilma would think."

"I really don't think it would be a problem."

"One step at a time."

Her heart filled with gladness, knowing her life was on

the right path. Many of her questions about her mother had been answered and she'd gotten to meet her grandmother. That had been an unexpected blessing.

Things weren't perfect. To be perfect in her world, Carter would've joined her Amish community and he would've had a good relationship with Wilma and the girls. She'd be working her orchard, the one she'd grown up on, and she and Carter would have children running around. "I should've found out who's looking after Betty. Who's paying for her to stay at the home."

"Self funded."

She stared at him. "Really?"

He nodded. "I found out while I was waiting for you. She also gets quite a few visitors."

"I must visit her again and then find out what I can … what we can do for her."

"I agree. You should get to know her as much as you can while she's still around."

"I've realized something," she said.

"What's that?"

"Life never stays the same. We're always moving away from some things and moving toward others."

"That's right. Just like in chess."

Florence laughed. "How's that like chess?"

"If you'd allow me to finish teaching you, then you'd know. Each piece has a part to play and they all interact together for the greater good. Will you let me teach you? You'd like it. It even has a bishop."

"A different kind, I'm sure." Inside she was still laughing, but she agreed. "Okay. Maybe then I'll know why you like it so much."

"I'll set up the board after our visit to the Jenkins' place."

"What, no app?"

"No, not when you have a real-life opponent."

She looked at him in surprise.

"Don't worry. We're not opponents. When you play chess with someone, you're really on the same side. We're creating something beautiful, masterful. We're affecting each other's destinies within the game."

She wondered if God was going to reach him through chess, somehow. "I never knew it was like that."

"You can think of the pawns as people and the other pieces as angels or demons. Maybe the king is God."

And there it was.

She gave thanks for her wonderful love-filled life, and then she looked forward to all the good things God had for their future. Not only would she get closer to her grandmother, she'd make the effort to find why Earl wasn't close to Wilma. Even if Wilma didn't want her around, there was no reason why she couldn't help repair the relationship between Earl and Wilma. Unless … something had happened that was unrepairable.

Her mind traveled back over what Betty had said. It sounded like the apple orchard had brought her parents together. That made it all the more important to get it back. And, get it back she would ... somehow.

I do hope you enjoyed The Englisher.

JOIN MY NEWSLETTER TO stay up to date with my new releases and special offers. I'll also send you two Amish romance books to download for free. Visit my website and join in the 'Newsletter' section.

https://samanthapriceauthor.com/

Samantha Price

THE AMISH BONNET SISTERS

Book 1
Amish Mercy

Book 2:
Amish Honor

Book 3
A Simple Kiss

Book 4
Amish Joy

Book 5
Amish Family Secrets

Book 6
The Englisher

Book 7
Missing Florence

THE NEXT BOOK IN THE SERIES:

Do you want to find out what happens to Florence, the apple orchard, and the bonnet sisters?

Book 7
Missing Florence

With two weddings to plan, It's a busy time for the Amish girls in the Baker family. Will their mother be successful in her desire to combine the weddings into a double?

When the new stepfather moves into the house, will he be harsh and strict like their new stepsister warned them?

Cherish is up to her usual mischief and drags one of her sisters with her.

Meanwhile, Florence is creating both the foundations of her new life and her new apple orchard.

When Florence gets to know her birth mother's family better, will she miss the Baker family all the more?

THE NEXT BOOK IN THE SERIES:

When another *Englisher* neighbor knocks on the door of the Baker home, is history about to repeat itself?

You will love this addition to the series because there is never a dull moment with the Amish Bonnet Sisters.

ABOUT THE AUTHOR

A prolific author of Amish fiction, Samantha Price wrote stories from a young age, but it wasn't until later in life that she took up writing full time. Formally an artist, she exchanged her paintbrush for the computer and, many best-selling book series later, has never looked back.

Samantha is happiest on her computer lost in the world of her characters.

To date, Samantha has received several All Stars Awards; Harlequin has published her Amish Love Blooms series, and Amazon Studios have produced several of her books in audio.

Samantha is best known for the Ettie Smith Amish Mysteries series and the Expectant Amish Widows series.

To learn more about Samantha Price and her books visit:

https://samanthapriceauthor.com/

Samantha Price loves to hear from her readers. Connect with her at:

samanthaprice333@gmail.com

www.facebook.com/SamanthaPriceAuthor

Follow Samantha Price on BookBub

Twitter @ AmishRomance